Praise for Johnny Townsend

In *Zombies for Jesus*, "Townsend isn't writing satire, but deeply emotional and revealing portraits of people who are, with a few exceptions, quite lovable."

> Kel Munger, *Sacramento News and Review*

Townsend's stories are "a gay *Portnoy's Complaint* of Mormonism. Salacious, sweet, sad, insightful, insulting, religiously ethnic, quirky-faithful, and funny."

> D. Michael Quinn, author of *The Mormon Hierarchy: Origins of Power*

Johnny Townsend is "an important voice in the Mormon community."

> Stephen Carter, editor of *Sunstone* magazine

"Told from a believably conversational first-person perspective, [*The Abominable Gayman*'s] novelistic focus on Anderson's journey to thoughtful self-acceptance allows for greater character development than often seen in short stories, which makes this well-paced work rich and satisfying, and one of Townsend's strongest. An extremely important contribution to the field of Mormon fiction." Named to Kirkus Reviews' Best of 2011.

Kirkus Reviews

"The thirteen stories in *Mormon Underwear* capture this struggle [between Mormonism and homosexuality] with humor, sadness, insight, and sometimes shocking details....*Mormon Underwear* provides compelling stories, literally from the inside-out."

Niki D'Andrea, *Phoenix New Times*

The Circumcision of God "asks questions that are not often asked out loud in Mormonism, and certainly not answered."

Jeff Laver, author of *Elder Petersen's Mission Memories*

"Townsend's lively writing style and engaging characters [in *Zombies for Jesus*] make for stories which force us to wake up, smell the (prohibited) coffee, and review our attitudes with regard to reading dogma so doggedly. These are tales which revel in the individual tics and quirks which make us human, Mormon or not, gay or not…"

       A.J. Kirby, The Short Review

In *Sex among the Saints,* "Townsend writes with a deadpan wit and a supple, realistic prose that's full of psychological empathy….he takes his protagonists' moral struggles seriously and invests them with real emotional resonance."

            Kirkus Reviews

"The Buzzard Tree," from *The Circumcision of God*, was listed as a finalist for the 2007 Whitney Award for Best Short LDS Fiction.

"The Rift," from *The Abominable Gayman*, is a "fascinating tale of an untenable situation…a *tour de force.*"

    David Lenson, editor, *The Massachusetts Review*

"Pronouncing the Apostrophe," from *The Golem of Rabbi Loew*, is "quiet and revealing, an intriguing tale…"

 Sima Rabinowitz, Literary Magazine Review, NewPages.com

"Johnny Townsend's short stories cannot be pigeon-holed. His keen observations on the human condition come in many shapes and sizes...reflecting on both his Jewish and Mormon backgrounds as well as life in the vast and varied American gay community. He dares to think and write about people and incidents that frighten away more timid artists. His perspective is sometimes startling, sometimes hilarious, sometimes poignant, but always compassionate."

Gerald S. Argetsinger, Artistic Director of the Hill Cumorah Pageant (1990-96)

The Circumcision of God is "a collection of short stories that consider the imperfect, silenced majority of Mormons, who may in fact be [the Church's] best hope....[The book leaves] readers regretting the church's willingness to marginalize those who best exemplify its ideals: those who love fiercely despite all obstacles, who brave challenges at great personal risk and who always choose the hard, higher road."

Kirkus Reviews

In *Mormon Fairy Tales*, Johnny Townsend displays "both a wicked sense of irony and a deep well of compassion."

Kel Munger, *Sacramento News and Review*

"*Selling the City of Enoch* exists at that awkward intersection where the LDS ideal meets the real world, and Townsend navigates his terrain with humor, insight, and pathos."

Donna Banta, author of *False Prophet*

The Golem of Rabbi Loew will prompt "gasps of outrage from conservative readers...a strong collection."

Kirkus Reviews

"That's one of the reasons why I found Johnny Townsend's new book *Mormon Fairy Tales* SO MUCH FUN!! Without fretting about what the theology is supposed to be if it were pinned down, Townsend takes you on a voyage to explore the rich-but-undertapped imagination of Mormonism. I loved his portrait of spirit prison! He really nailed it—not in an official doctrine sort of way, but in a sort of 'if you know Mormonism, you know this is what it must be like' way—and what a prison it is!

Johnny Townsend has written at least ten books of Mormon stories. So far, I've read only two (*Mormon Fairy Tales* and *The Circumcision of God*), but I'm planning to read the rest—and you should too, if you'd like a fun and interesting new perspective on Mormons in life and imagination!"

C. L. Hanson, *Main Street Plaza*

Zombies for Jesus is "eerie, erotic, and magical."

Publishers Weekly

"While [Townsend's] many touching vignettes draw deeply from Mormon mythology, history, spirituality and culture, [*Mormon Fairy Tales*] is neither a gaudy act of proselytism nor angry protest literature from an ex-believer. Like all good fiction, his stories are simply about the joys, the hopes and the sorrows of people."

Kirkus Reviews

"In *Let the Faggots Burn* author Johnny Townsend restores this tragic event [the UpStairs Lounge fire] to its proper place in LGBT history and reminds us that the victims of the blaze were not just 'statistics,' but real people with real lives, families, and friends."

Jesse Monteagudo, The Bilerico Project

Marginal Mormons is "an irreverent, honest look at life outside the mainstream Mormon Church....Throughout his musings on sin and forgiveness, Townsend beautifully demonstrates his characters' internal, perhaps irreconcilable struggles....Rather than anger and disdain, he offers an honest portrayal of people searching for meaning and community in their lives, regardless of their life choices or secrets." Named to Kirkus Reviews' Best of 2012.

Kirkus Reviews

"The Sneakover Prince" from *God's Gargoyles* is "one of the most sweet and romantic stor[ies] I have ever read."

Elisa Rolle, Reviews and Ramblings, founder of The Rainbow Awards

"*Let the Faggots Burn* is a one-of-a-kind piece of history. Without Townsend's diligence and devotion, many details would've been lost forever. With his tremendous foresight and tenacious research, Townsend put a face on this tragedy at a time when few people would talk about it....Through Townsend's vivid writing, you will sense what it must've been like in those final moments as the fire ripped through the UpStairs Lounge. *Let the Faggots Burn* is a chilling and insightful glimpse into a largely forgotten and ignored chapter of LGBT history."

Robert Camina, writer and producer of the documentary *Raid of the Rainbow Lounge*

The stories in *The Mormon Victorian Society* "register the new openness and confidence of gay life in the age of same-sex marriage....What hasn't changed is Townsend's wry, conversational prose, his subtle evocations of character and social dynamics, and his deadpan humor. His warm empathy still glows in this intimate yet clear-eyed engagement with Mormon theology and folkways. Funny, shrewd and finely wrought dissections of the awkward contradictions—and surprising harmonies—between conscience and desire." Named to Kirkus Reviews' Best of 2013.

Kirkus Reviews

"Johnny Townsend's 'Partying with St. Roch' [in the anthology *Latter-Gay Saints*] tells a beautiful, haunting tale."

Kent Brintnall, Out in Print: Queer Book Reviews

"The struggles and solutions of the individuals [in *Latter-Gay Saints*] will resonate across faith traditions and help readers better understand the cost of excluding gay members from full religious participation."

Publishers Weekly

"This collection of short stories [*The Mormon Victorian Society*] featuring gay Mormon characters slammed in the face from the first page, wrestled my heart and mind to the floor, and left me panting and wanting more by the end. Johnny Townsend has created so many memorable characters in such few pages. I went weeks thinking about this book. It truly touched me."

Tom Webb, judge for The Rainbow Awards (A Bear on Books)

Dragons of the Book of Mormon is an "entertaining collection….Townsend's prose is sharp, clear, and easy to read, and his characters are well rendered…"

Publishers Weekly

"The pre-eminent documenter of alternative Mormon lifestyles…Townsend has a deep understanding of his characters, and his limpid prose, dry humor and well-grounded (occasionally magical) realism make their spiritual conundrums both compelling and entertaining. [*Dragons of the Book of Mormon* is] [a]nother of Townsend's critical but affectionate and absorbing tours of Mormon discontent." Named to Kirkus Reviews' Best of 2014.

Kirkus Reviews

"Mormon Movie Marathon," from *Selling the City of Enoch*, "is funny, constructively critical, but also sad because the desire…for belonging is so palpable."

Levi S. Peterson, author of *The Backslider* and *The Canyons of Grace*

In *Let the Faggots Burn*, "Townsend's heart-rending descriptions of the victims...seem to [make them] come alive once more."

       Kit Van Cleave, *OutSmart Magazine*

Selling the City of Enoch is "sharply intelligent...pleasingly complex...The stories are full of...doubters, but there's no vindictiveness in these pages; the characters continuously poke holes in Mormonism's more extravagant absurdities, but they take very little pleasure in doing so....Many of Townsend's stories...have a provocative edge to them, but this [book] displays a great deal of insight as well...a playful, biting and surprisingly warm collection."

              Kirkus Reviews

Gayrabian Nights is "an allegorical tour de force...a hard-core emotional punch."

         Gay. Guy. Reading and Friends

In *Gayrabian Nights*, "Townsend's prose is always limpid and evocative, and...he finds real drama and emotional depth in the most ordinary of lives."

              Kirkus Reviews

Gayrabian Nights is a "complex revelation of how seriously soul damaging the denial of the true self can be."

        Ryan Rhodes, author of *Free Electricity*

In *Lying for the Lord*, Townsend "gets under the skin of his characters to reveal their complexity and conflicts....shrewd, evocative [and] wryly humorous."

        Kirkus Reviews

Despots of Deseret

Johnny Townsend

Copyright © 2015 Johnny Townsend

ISBN 978-1-63490-342-4

All rights reserved. No part of this publication may be reproduced, stored in a retrieval system, or transmitted in any form or by any means, electronic, mechanical, recording, or otherwise, without the prior written permission of the author.

Printed in the United States of America on acid-free paper.

This book is a work of fiction. Names, characters, events, and dialogue are the product of the author's imagination or are used fictitiously. Any resemblance to actual persons, living or dead, is entirely coincidental.

BookLocker.com, Inc.
2015

First Edition

Cover design by Todd Engel

"Satan…wins a great victory when he can get members of the Church to…do their own thinking….When our leaders speak, the thinking has been done….To think otherwise, without immediate repentance, may cost one his faith…and leave him a stranger to the kingdom of God."

Improvement Era

"When the Prophet speaks…the debate is over."

Ensign

"I would rather have questions that can't be answered than answers that can't be questioned."

Richard Feynman

Dedicated to those coerced to take part in electroshock torture at Brigham Young University

Special thanks to Donna Banta
for her editorial assistance

Contents

Too Nice 1
The Sunday After 9
Called to Condemn 18
Still True 26
Teacher of the Millennium 34
Sealed with a Kiss 43
The Dinner Party 60
Patty Lou Soils Herself 69
To Serve God 79
Best Christian Example 91
Christmas Brownies 100
Poison Ivy Testimonies 110
A Stupor of Thought 120
Reverse Engineering 131
Sweating Bullets 139
The Contract 148
Third Time's the Charm 158
Your Mission, If You Choose To Accept It 169
Books by Johnny Townsend 181

Too Nice

"You're such a nice guy, Kirby," said Elaine after I set the files on her desk.

The words filled me with shame and pride and disgust. And anger. I smiled pleasantly at Elaine. "It's no problem," I replied. Walking back to my cubicle, I wondered again if I was ever going to be normal. I was twenty-seven years old now. Over two decades had passed. Was this obsession never going to end?

Logging onto my computer, I pulled up my supply order for the section and added a last item. Elaine needed a new bottle of hand sanitizer. She hadn't said anything, but I'd noticed when I was at her desk, and our supply cabinet was getting low. I'd make the order tomorrow.

I spent the next hour or so working quietly at my computer, blotting out personal thoughts, until it was time for my break. "I'm heading over to Bartell's," I announced to the others in the department. "Anyone need anything?"

I felt as an obese man must, loving every bite of every doughnut while at the same time despising myself for eating them. I hated that I felt this compulsion to help, but I also loved the smiles and gratitude I received from other people, really just the idea that I was easing someone else's burdens, however slightly and briefly. I felt like a failure for experiencing this desire. But I knew it would be more of a failure to give in and no longer try to help others.

Why did going to a drugstore have to be such a major moral issue?

I hated my mother for what she'd done.

And yet, maybe she'd helped me. Perhaps it was because of her that I wasn't like everybody else.

I brought back a Coke and a bag of chips and a boiled egg for my coworkers and sat down to continue working. Cynthia interrupted me to ask a question about compliance regulations, and I stopped what I was doing to help. She had only been with the company six months and was still struggling to fully learn her position and duties. She'd come a long way, but some of the others grew irritated that she didn't know everything already. I looked at her now, dim comprehension fighting to take control of her face. She still didn't understand what I'd just explained.

"I can set aside thirty minutes on Friday to go over all this with you more fully," I said. I'd given her mini-lessons in addition to her regular training twice already.

"Thank you, Kirby, I'd appreciate it."

Cynthia smiled and returned to her desk, but I sat thinking a moment longer. What the woman really needed was confidence. I opened up a new email to the Nominating Committee for Employee of the Month and took a few minutes to write a case for giving the next award to Cynthia, pointing out her strong points and how quickly she'd adapted to her new job and become a contributing member of the department. It was all true enough, though I doubted many others saw it that way, including Cynthia. I CC'ed our manager and Cynthia and hit Send.

I returned to my work, putting Cynthia out of my mind. I answered a few phone calls from irritated vendors and made an effort to smooth out the problems. I looked at my calendar and saw an endless future of empty days ahead of me.

A ping told me I'd received a new email. "You are so kind," was all Cynthia said. The words filled me with shame and pride and disgust. And anger. I could hear a soft sniffling coming from her cubicle. I returned to my work.

Things often slowed down right at the end of the day, and we all found more time to talk to each other. Peter brought up the Superbowl loss of the Seahawks last week, but that topic was nipped pretty quickly. Elaine mentioned being diagnosed with diabetes recently and needing to lose weight. I was glad I was in good shape. "I'll walk with you during lunch if that helps," I said.

"You're so sweet," she replied.

Then Fred said something about installing a new security system at his house. "It's a waste of money," said Marcus.

"That's because you're a man," said Cynthia. "I certainly feel like I need one."

An old memory came flooding back, and I debated whether or not to share. "When I was a kid," I said, "and my father left us, my mother started putting chairs in front of the door so we'd hear someone breaking in."

Everyone chuckled.

"She put the coffee table on the stairs, and she made my sister and me sleep in her bed with her."

"A little overprotective, was she?" said Peter, smiling.

"No," I said coldly. "She wasn't that."

I could see the puzzled looks from my change in tone, and I felt guilty.

"What was she if not overprotective?" asked Peter.

"Afraid," I replied. There were more puzzled looks, and we got back to work.

At 5:00, it was time to leave, and I held the door open for Elaine, since we were both exiting at the same time. I turned my face upward to feel the tiny raindrops. Everyone else downtown was hurrying along the sidewalks in the light rain, but this was my favorite time of day, so I strolled casually. Freedom, I thought. It was the only taste of it I got in life, and it lasted all too short a time. I looked at the others bustling around me and wondered what it would be like to be normal.

If normal people were insulated and uncaring, was it really good to be normal?

I hated being grateful to my mother.

I only had to wait at the Pioneer Square station for a few minutes before the light rail pulled up. A middle-aged woman struggled to get her rolling suitcase on board, so I took care of it, directing her to the bicycle stall so she'd be out of the way of other passengers, both for her benefit and theirs.

She looked as if she thought I might rob her. I walked to the other end of the car.

Dear God, I thought, if you really exist, please send me some help. I really need your help. I don't know what to do with my life any more.

I looked about at the other riders. One heavy white woman was reading a Kindle. A balding Indian man was reading an actual book. A few of the younger people were poking at their cell phones. A Latina woman leaned against the window, sleeping.

Dear God, I thought, you can be nice too, can't you? Please help me.

I stepped off the train at the Rainier Beach station and crossed the street to the bus stop. A mentally disabled Asian teenager stood there, picking his nose while an elderly black woman with a stroller stared blankly at the street. The 106 pulled up shortly, and I found a seat behind an old white man in a wheelchair with long, stringy hair. He was berating his wife every few seconds. She looked out the window.

I turned away and saw a Latina woman in her thirties caressing the hair of her eight-year-old daughter in another seat across the aisle.

I hadn't spoken to my mother in years. I hadn't even wanted to see her after she was released from prison, but my foster parents insisted, though I couldn't imagine why, after what she'd done to me.

Please, God.

We passed Kubota Garden, and I pulled the cord hanging over the window. I made my way past the wheelchair and stood just behind the yellow line at the front of the bus. When the driver opened the doors, I turned to her and said, "Thank you," as sincerely as possible and stepped off the bus.

I could see my neighbor Zenobia struggling with her recycling bin as I walked up to the house. I said hello and helped her get it to the curb. "How are the kids?" I asked.

"Oh, just fine. Thank you so much, Kirby. You're such a nice guy."

I closed my eyes.

I unlocked my front door, picked up the key to the mail box, and retrieved my mail. Four solicitations for charities I'd given to recently, asking for still more money. I felt both irritated and guilty at the same time.

I changed out of my work attire, ate a salad I'd bought at Safeway the night before, and sat on the sofa to watch Rachel Maddow. Now there was a woman with a purpose to her life.

I wished I had a purpose.

Was my purpose just to be nice? To be nice despite what my mother had done? Or was my purpose to finally forget what had happened? Nice people didn't hold grudges.

But how could I forget?

Every single day of my life, I remembered how the woman had continually criticized me for being too nice, saying one day I'd regret it. I remembered how when I was six years old, a man had asked me to help him look for his dog. I remembered how he'd taken me, tied me up, taped my mouth, and told me, "You'll never see your mommy again." I remembered how he'd hit me and threatened me and terrorized me for hours.

I remembered when my mother and grandmother and aunt came to pick me up from the man they'd hired, asking me if I'd finally learned my lesson about being too nice.

Mostly, I'd remembered how, even at that tender young age, I realized I had a decision to make. Would I let my mother's "lesson" change me, or would I continue to try to be the nice boy I'd always wanted to be?

I glanced over at my cell phone and then turned back to Rachel.

A short while later, there was a knock at my door. Looking through the peephole, I could see a black man in his early twenties. It had been dark outside for over an hour. What could the man possibly want? I thought of the string of neighborhood robberies in the past few weeks.

"Can I help you?" I asked, opening the door.

"I'm selling subscriptions to the *Seattle Times*," he said, holding up a newspaper. He went on to tell me how many weeks I could get and for what price. I didn't really need the newspaper, but I gave him some money, and he took down my name and address and walked away.

I sat back down to watch the rest of Rachel.

My life felt so empty.

During a commercial, I went to the kitchen to grab a handful of roasted almonds. There was another knock at the door. I walked cautiously back and looked out the peephole again. There were two young men, both white, wearing white shirts and ties. I opened the door.

"Can I help you?" I asked.

"Good evening, sir," said one of the young men. "Have you ever asked yourself the questions, 'Where did I come from? Why am I here? Where am I going when this life is over?'" He looked at me eagerly, smiling. The other young man was smiling as well.

They looked nice.

I read their nametags and saw the books they were holding. Mormons, I thought. The guys who believed so strongly in families.

I turned to look briefly at my cell phone on the shelf near the door.

"Is it nice to forgive someone who doesn't deserve it?" I asked.

The two young men looked at each other in confusion, and then they began smiling brightly again. "If you have a few minutes," the first one said, "we have a message we'd like to share with you."

I sighed and stood there for a long moment looking at them. Then I nodded and let them in.

The Sunday After

It was the first Sunday of the New Year. Last week, the tsunami had killed almost a quarter of a million people. I still hadn't heard word from my niece who was vacationing in Thailand. I'd started my fast right at midnight on New Year's Eve, twelve hours earlier than usual, hoping the extra hours would help persuade Heavenly Father to show mercy on Tabitha.

What could mercy possibly mean to a god who had just killed so many people?

I hadn't gone to church in a few months, so I wasn't sure Heavenly Father was going to listen to my prayers in any event, no matter how long I fasted. But what else could I do? I was in touch with my sister Amber, who was literally waiting by her phone hour after hour, staring at the landline on the end table, her cell phone in her hand. Charles was on his own phone making calls to every agency he could think of, but my sister accepted no calls from friends or family, trying to keep her lines clear, sending out two emails a day to let us know she was sure Tabitha would be phoning any minute.

Amber had stopped going to church three years ago, so she wouldn't be at Fast and Testimony meeting with me today. Tabitha had flown to Thailand with a girlfriend from college, church the last thing on her mind.

Not *a* girlfriend. *Her* girlfriend.

Would Heavenly Father spare a lesbian?

I looked in the mirror and straightened my tie. No matter how many years I'd been tying the damn things, I still couldn't do it without a mirror in front of me. I hadn't had to wear one at work in years, but church services still required the accessory.

I saw the reflection of the freshly made bed in the glass, and my shoulders slumped. Six months had passed since the divorce became final. Erin had even insisted on a temple divorce to ensure I couldn't "recapture" her in the next life. She'd moved to another stake. The two kids were both finished college and married, living their own lives in other cities.

The house was so big.

I picked up my scriptures and headed out the door, obeying the speed limit on the ten-minute drive to church. Sunday was the only day I paid attention to the speedometer. The parking lot was almost full by the time I pulled in, but I found a space at the far end and started walking toward the front entrance. I nodded at Brother Higgins and his wife. He nodded politely but she looked at me with her lips set a little tight.

It's not as if I'd committed adultery or anything. I'd just told Erin I wasn't sure I believed anymore. It wasn't as if I didn't still love her, despite our differences. And though I never gave her all the children she wanted, she had never tried to get pregnant elsewhere. That had to say something about her character. But my no longer believing was simply more than she could bear.

I looked up at the windows high up on the chapel wall. I had to make myself believe today. For Tabitha's sake.

"Good morning, Jake," I said to one of the other high priests as I entered the foyer.

"Welcome back," he said with a friendly smile. "It's good to see you starting the New Year off right." He grabbed my hand and squeezed hard.

I forced a smile back.

"Hi, Jake," said Brother Robertson, the Gospel Doctrine teacher, pushing past two other men to reach me. He clapped me on the back. "We've missed you."

"And my questions?"

Brother Robertson laughed heartily. "Well, we've *mostly* missed you."

I wasn't going to be a pain in the butt today, I decided. I needed whatever brownie points I could get. "I'm looking forward to your class after Fast and Testimony."

"It'll be a good one today, for sure."

I shook Bishop Franklin's hand next and then moved on into the chapel. For the past few years, I'd been sitting closer and closer to the back, but today I sat in the fourth row, right in the center, not in either of the two side sections. "I'm engaged, Heavenly Father," I prayed. "I'm engaged. I'm trying. Please help Tabitha and her girlfriend. Please." I checked my phone to make sure it was on vibrate. There were no texts from Amber.

The Killian family sat in the row ahead of me: husband, wife, and five children. The Raleighs sat a few spaces away: husband, wife, and four children.

Erin and I only had the two. Erin always wanted more, had said so right from the start, but I'd insisted on using condoms pretty early on. It probably wasn't fair of me to make the decision unilaterally, so I understood that Erin was justified in being miffed. Ten years into our marriage, I'd noticed a speck on one of the condom packages. In some back corner of my mind, I remembered I'd seen specks on several of the other packages before, and for some reason, I was finally curious enough to look at it under the light, realizing then to my horror it was a pin prick. Erin had inserted a pin through each of the condoms, hoping one strong swimmer would find its way to success. I never said anything but instead started wearing two condoms. It didn't do much for me sensually, but I didn't need more children to have a forever family.

Or maybe I did. My family certainly hadn't lasted forever.

Was Tabitha still sealed to Amber and Charles, I wondered? No one had been excommunicated officially, of course. They'd just become "inactive." I wondered if there was any god out there to recognize temple rituals in the first place. Was Tabitha gone forever?

Please, Heavenly Father. I'll believe again. I will. Please help us.

The organist seemed to be playing music that was more somber than usual. But then, she played so slowly even on good days that any normally upbeat music often sounded dreary. Finally, though, the bishop stood up to start the meeting. "Welcome to all on this fine, beautiful morning. I hope everyone is starting their New Year on the right foot. Let's keep all our resolutions, to make it to church every single Sunday of the year, to read the scriptures every single day, to have Family Home Evening every Monday night, to pay our tithing regularly." He smiled beatifically out at the congregation. "We have a few announcements before we begin." The man proceeded to mention several thoroughly uninteresting events coming up, and then told us what opening hymn we'd be singing, and who would be offering the opening prayer.

Odd that he hadn't mentioned the tsunami or asked us to keep all those affected in our prayers. Amber had told me specifically that she'd called her Home Teachers. "I may need some Church connections to get a flight out for Tabitha," she explained to me. "Who knows? I'll sell my soul for Tabitha."

We sang "We Thank Thee O God for a Prophet" and then Sister Williams offered the opening prayer. She was a sweet old woman, one of the members everyone loved. Surely, she'd ask Heavenly Father for a special blessing. I bowed my head.

Nothing. When she finished, I looked up quizzically and followed her off the stage with my eyes. How strange, I thought. Did no one watch the news? The tsunami had been on the air every night for the past week.

Well, I'm here to do *my* part, I reminded myself. I'm fasting. I'm attending services. I'm being a good boy. Heavenly Father, please have mercy. I looked upward toward the vaulted ceiling.

I remembered Tabitha's last visit to my house, two weeks before her trip. I saw my niece more often than my own children, who Erin had long ago turned against me, well before the divorce. "You're better off, Uncle Jake," she said. "Even *I* was never attracted to Erin."

I'd smiled wistfully.

She punched me in the shoulder. "Oh, cheer up, Uncle Jake. If push comes to shove, I know a few women who swing both ways. I could set you up sometime." Then she smiled mischievously and added, "I know some hot guys, too. You'd never have to worry about pregnancy again." She knew of my long-standing battle with Erin. Of course, that had been a moot point the last several years after menopause had entered the relationship. But Erin had never let me or anyone else in the family forget that I'd deprived her of all the spirit children for whom she was destined to provide bodies.

"Thanks, honey," I'd replied. "A bisexual woman will do just fine. I'm free this Saturday at 8:00. Ask her if she's willing to stay over. Maybe bring a friend?"

Erin had looked shocked for a moment until she realized I was joking. "It's been quite a while since you've joked, Uncle Jake. That's a good sign."

A good sign.

I looked at my watch as we began singing the sacrament hymn. There'd been no sign of Tabitha for a week. Was she lying unconscious in some dilapidated hospital? Maybe her legs were broken. Had she cracked some ribs? I'd seen footage of people with terrible gashes in their arms and legs, on their faces. Had she been disfigured? Had she actually lost a limb, had to undergo amputation to save her life? Perhaps she was fighting to stay with us every minute, wondering why we weren't there to help her. Feeling abandoned.

Was she clinging to life, using the last of her energy to mourn Colleen? Please, Heavenly Father, let Tabitha keep the will to live.

After the sacrament was passed, the bishop opened the floor to anyone who wanted to bear their testimony. Even back in my believing days, this had always been the most excruciating meeting of the month. And that was saying something. Sister Richards was always the first to rise. She never walked to the podium, having suffered a stroke twenty years ago and being virtually paralyzed on her left side. She stood and started speaking, not waiting for the microphone which one of the deacons hurried to her pew.

"I just want to take this opportunity to say that I know the Church is true. I took too long while listening to the missionaries, straddling the fence, not wanting to leave my former church. And Heavenly Father was gracious and gave me a stroke to let me know he wanted me to hurry up and make a decision. I was baptized as soon as I could stand again. And I've borne my testimony every single month since. I want to say again that I know the Church is true. Joseph Smith was a prophet of God. The Book of Mormon is the word of God. Anyone who doubts God's presence in our lives, just look at this walker." She slapped the metal frame. "I say this in the name of Jesus Christ. Amen." She plopped back down in her pew.

Sister Richards was followed by a blond six-year-old girl who walked to the podium and had to stand on a box to reach the microphone. "I know the Church is true," she whispered, looking out at her parents and covering her mouth to hide a giggle. "I know the Book of Mormon is true. I love my family. And I say this in the name of Jesus Christ. Amen." When she said it, it sounded like "cheese and rice."

Next came Brother Carlton. He also liked speaking regularly on Fast and Testimony day. I took a quick peek at my phone to make sure I hadn't missed any texts. Nothing, dammit. Please, Heavenly Father, have pity. Pity. "Brothers and Sisters," Brother Carlton began, "I had a profound experience this week I want to tell you all about. I was walking downtown, and there were lots of panhandlers and bums. One woman came up to me, her hair filthy, dirt on her face. She held out her hand, and I said, 'I'll give you some money if you'll answer a question honestly.' She nodded, and I asked, 'What do you know about the Mormon Church? Would you like to know more?' I was sure I could help her more by giving her the gospel than by giving her money to buy liquor." He shook his head. "And do you know what she said to me?" He paused and looked out at the congregation searchingly. "She said, 'I used to *be* Mormon, but I started drinking, and I ended up on the streets. Tell everyone to stay true.'" Brother Carlton smiled broadly. It seemed unlikely to me that any homeless woman would have said those words, but who knew? Brother Carlton followed this with the standard testimony and then returned to his seat.

More testimonies followed, by a couple of teenagers trying to compete with each other for holiest teen, by a young mother holding her baby, by a couple of the older women, by another six-year-old whose mother whispered in her ear what to say. I didn't feel the Spirit with any of them, though. The Holy Ghost wasn't testifying to me that what I was hearing was true. I felt disappointed. Perhaps that meant I was too far gone. And if that were the case, there was no reason for Heavenly Father to answer my prayers. Or Amber's. She was even further gone than I was. She was an atheist to my agnosticism.

Heavenly Father, don't the heathen deserve your pity, too? Tabitha still believes in you, even if she isn't Mormon. Forget about us. Just help *her*.

And Colleen.

Amber was in touch with Colleen's parents, too. But they hadn't had any contact from Colleen ever since they'd disowned her, so there wasn't much hope for news there.

The meeting dragged on, no longer than usual, but each minute feeling like fifteen. Finally, though, the bishop stood up again and announced the closing hymn and the closing prayer. We sang "Let Us Oft Speak Kind Words" and then Brother Bartlett offered the benediction.

As the other congregants started to stand and move off to Sunday School, I continued to sit, staring at the pulpit. Not a single person had even mentioned the tsunami today. No prayers had been offered for the injured or the families who lost loved ones. No one said one measly word about possibly the largest natural disaster in recorded history in any of their accounts of thanksgiving to the Lord. Were we all living on the same planet?

I picked up my scriptures and followed everyone out of the chapel. Brother Robertson shook my hand as I reached the foyer again. Even though he had to start teaching in a few minutes, he always made sure to greet everyone a second time. "We're still in the Relief Society room," he reminded me, as if I'd forgotten the location for the class in three short months.

I stared at him and then looked at all the other smiling people in the foyer.

"What is wrong with all of you?" I asked.

"Huh?" said Brother Robertson, surprised.

"Here," I said, handing him my Bible and my triple combination. "Maybe you can find some use for these."

I walked out through the front doors and made my way back to the car. A few other people were ducking out early as well, skipping the rest of services so they could break their fast ahead of schedule. I sat down and turned on the car radio to hear the news. I checked my phone again for messages.

Then I put my head down on the steering wheel and cried.

Called to Condemn

"So, Russell, what do you think?" asked Bishop Hamilton, peering at me from behind his desk. "Are you willing to accept the Lord's call to serve?"

I looked back at the bishop, confused. I had served as a missionary in Scotland for two years as I was expected to do. Upon returning to Seattle and enrolling at the University of Washington, I had accepted a calling as Sunday School teacher for the 14- and 15-year-olds. That had lasted three years, until my graduation. After I began my MA program in English literature, I was called to be second counselor in the Elders Quorum, where I also taught Priesthood lessons twice a month. That was my current calling.

And those types of callings I understood. My father had been first counselor in the stake presidency when I was in high school. My mother had served in the Relief Society. My sister Gretchen was serving in the Primary right now. It was a given that Mormons led a life of service. When the bishop called you—when the *Lord* called you—you accepted and did what you needed to do.

But this?

"I don't know, Bishop," I said slowly. "I'll have to think about it."

"*Think* about it?" asked Bishop Hamilton as if talking to a five-year-old. "Or *pray* about it?"

"I need to do both, Bishop."

He leaned back in his chair and touched the tips of his fingers together as if enclosing an invisible softball. His brows furrowed, and he frowned. "I just don't understand, Russell," he said. "You're one of our best members. Stalwart. Strong. That's why the Lord is giving you this special assignment. And you being an English major, it's perfect for you."

I wasn't quite sure how to put my concerns into words. English major or not, I was speechless. "It just seems so—so sneaky," I mumbled.

"The scriptures tell us to be as cunning as foxes in order to fight the evil in the world. Your father was in the stake presidency. Surely, you're aware that we keep close tabs on members who are straying." He looked at me intently. "We have one of the high priests do a stakeout to see if a sister is having an affair. We have an elder from the Elders Quorum follow a married man suspected of being gay to see if he goes to a gay bar. We have people read all the anti-Mormon blogs to get information on people. We read the Mormon blogs, too. We have someone monitor Amazon to see when new books about Mormons are being written." He held out his hands.

"And that's where I come in."

"Exactly."

I took a deep breath and tried to accept the inevitable. "But you don't want me to actually read these books on the list," I said, holding up the paper he'd handed me earlier.

"Heavens, no!" The bishop laughed. "Satan is cunning, too. You don't want to get sucked into apostasy. You just need to write reviews on Amazon for the six books on the list, persuade other Mormons not to read them. Heavenly Father needs you to help protect his flock."

"Well, what's one little review going to do?" I asked, shrugging.

Bishop Hamilton laughed again. "The Lord doesn't put all his eggs in one basket, young man. There are several bishops having this same conversation with other saints across the country right at this very moment. Together, we can destroy any chance those evil 'authors' have of dragging others to Outer Darkness with them."

The bishop looked at me intently again. My eyes dropped to the paper in my hand.

"Will you do the Lord's will, Russell?" he asked. "Will you accept your calling as Member Security Officer?"

"Isn't—isn't it lying to write a bad review without even reading the book?" I asked.

Now the bishop started to look angry. "We're *telling* you the books are bad," he said firmly. "So now you *know* they are. It isn't a lie to follow your leaders."

I sighed again. Interviews with bishops and stake presidents were supposed to be confidential, but I knew that Bishop Hamilton had told my father I'd confessed to masturbation, because my father had come to my apartment to have a serious man-to-man talk with me, asking me to join the Sons of Helaman support group. If I didn't agree to the bishop's request now, he'd report me again, and the relationship with my father was strained enough as it was, first, because I hadn't wanted to go to Brigham Young University, and second, because I was in no hurry to marry.

There were third and fourth and fifth reasons, too. I didn't need to add a sixth.

"Okay, Bishop," I said, nodding. "I'll do it."

"The Lord will bless you, Russell." He reached over and shook my hand, and then I turned around to leave.

I drove back to my apartment slowly, looking at all the other young adults on the streets in the University district. Even in the cool spring weather, the girls wore sleeveless tops. Tight tops. Both they and the boys they hung out with were smoking and laughing. Probably on their way to drink beer somewhere as well.

The college years were hard on young Mormons. So many of us finally had full access to the Internet for the first time. We were learning uncomfortable truths in class, lies about the Church online. If I could save just a few of the others by writing these reviews, it seemed the least I could do.

Be as cunning as foxes.

I walked up the stairs to my second-floor apartment and unlocked the door. *Tess of the D'Urbervilles* lay on my coffee table. I really enjoyed 19th century British literature, from Jane Austen to Charles Dickens to Wilkie Collins to Thomas Hardy to Sir Arthur Conan Doyle to the Bronte sisters and most of the others as well. The problem was finding time to read everything. When one took a poetry class, most of the poems were pretty short, but when one specialized in fiction, the reading load was almost too heavy to bear.

And now I had to read these six additional books.

Well, I *didn't* have to read them. That was the whole point. All I had to do was write a few lines, maybe a short paragraph, about each book. I was used to writing a fifteen- or twenty-page research paper every week or two. I could certainly muster six paragraphs.

I turned on my computer and went to Amazon. I looked at the list the bishop had given me and typed in the first title. *Secret Combinations.* I read the blurb. It seemed to be about Mormons spying on each other.

I felt very uncomfortable.

I typed in the second title. *Court of Love*. This one was about a vindictive bishop who sets out to excommunicate a young woman who refuses to stop talking about wanting to hold the priesthood.

The Unholy of Holies was about secret, evil rituals that went on behind closed doors in the temple by the leaders of the Church.

The bishop was right. This crap deserved whatever scathing words I could think of. And it looked like most of these books were self-published. They were probably awful even apart from their content.

The Pro-Anti-Nephi-Lehies simply made fun of anyone who believed the Book of Mormon was true. *Vampires of the Blood Atonement* brought up the lie that the Church used to kill apostates by shedding their blood in order to save their souls. But it did it in a supposedly humorous way so that it wouldn't seem like the author was being as venomous as he actually was.

Finally, the last book was *The Tyranny of Silence*. I started to read the blurb, hoping to gather enough information to jot down some ideas for my review. But I was drawn back to the cover over on the left side of the screen. The front showed a woman's face, Photoshopped so that her mouth was missing. There was a button on the Amazon page that let me flip to the back cover, which showed the lower half of a man's face, with a heavy five o'clock shadow, the man's lips sewn together with thick, crisscrossing thread.

I was angry. The Church didn't try to keep people silent, I thought. If anything, Mormons talked too much. Like the bishop blabbing my sins to my father every chance he got.

I turned back to the blurb. This was the story of a young married couple who discover truths online about the Church that the Church tried to keep hidden. When they begin asking questions in Gospel Doctrine class, they are called in to see the bishop, who tells them they will be disciplined if they continue to make other members doubt. When the bishop monitors their library cards through a member who works for the public library and learns the two are reading damning history books about the early Church, he disfellowships them, dismissing them from all of their callings and not letting them speak up in class or in Sacrament meeting. Finally, the couple begin spying on the bishop and end up going public with the scandals they find out about him.

These writers must have lost their souls, I thought. Maybe they'd literally sold those souls to Satan in order to publish, thinking they'd become rich and famous.

My reviews could help nip that dream in the bud.

Though I had to admit, I'd occasionally had the same fantasy about my own bishop. Surely, he had some secrets he wouldn't want blabbed to *his* family members.

Thank goodness I'd never confessed my darkest secret, that not only did I enjoy 19th century British lit, but I also enjoyed written porn of the period as well. I'd read *The Romance of Lust* three times already. Sometimes, I even fantasized about slipping a copy into the bishop's briefcase and then tipping off Sister Hamilton anonymously.

The Sons of Helaman was not helping me nearly enough. I looked back at the computer. This special calling was a blessing. It was giving me the chance to make up for so many of my awful sins. If I could help other people avoid sin, perhaps the Lord would be more willing to forgive my own.

And I could be blistering. Academia had certainly taught me that. I could skewer these six authors and make them regret ever putting pen to paper in an attempt to discredit the Church.

Murder was a sin, but killing in self-defense or during war was not. Being cruel to these apostates was no more cruelty than killing a Nazi was. And there was no doubt that there was a war between good and evil here in the Last Days. This drivel proved it.

I was going to be good.

I reread the blurb and started writing down notes and ideas for my review, smiling, grateful now the bishop had called me to his office. He knew this was going to help me become stronger. The *Lord* knew. Maybe I'd even give up masturbating tonight when I went to bed. I might even share this technique with others from the Sons of Helaman, get them to input some reviews as well. I supposed the call really needed to come from the bishop, but we were always told to be "anxiously engaged in a good cause." And it was a support group, after all. If I could offer support, I was going to do it. That would make me stronger as well.

And maybe the damn bishop would finally stop tattling on me to my father.

I looked again at the image of the front cover, the woman's face without the mouth. I flipped again to the back and looked at the man with his mouth sewn shut.

Then I read the blurb one more time.

The print book cost $12.95, but the ebook was only $1.99. Seemed the author was really mostly interested in seeing that his book was read, not in making money. Financial greed wasn't the only kind of greed out there, obviously. Greed for the souls of men was even more wicked.

But the book actually sounded interesting. I would never really spy on my bishop, but it might be fun to read about someone else doing it.

Russell, you don't have time for this nonsense, I told myself. You have two more hours of homework tonight that absolutely has to be done. Get a grip.

I looked at the woman's face again, and I felt a small stirring in my groin.

I turned to look toward *Tess* lying out on the coffee table and sighed. Then I pulled out my debit card and downloaded the abominable text. I could get even more ammo for my review if I read at least a few chapters, I thought. Specifics always carried more weight.

I turned on my Kindle and began to read.

Still True

I wished I were a movie director. One of my favorite films was *Groundhog Day*. Justin and I used to watch it at least once a year, though never in February. On our second date, after we'd just watched the movie for the first time, he said to me, "Fletcher, that's the way eternity is going to be for us. We'll get to redo everything as many times as it takes till we get everything right."

"Reincarnation?" I asked.

"No. Just practice. Practice makes perfect, and we're commanded to be perfect."

I must have frowned in response because he then added, "Fletcher, we'll get to make love for the first time a million times. We'll have our first kiss a million more. And you'll hear me say 'I love you' with this same intensity a million more times beyond that."

I laughed. "You love me? Justin, it's only our second date."

He took my hand and looked deep into my eyes. "Are you telling me you don't feel the same way?"

I stared back into his eyes and knew he was right. We both lived in Salt Lake but had never met until a Sunstone symposium a few weeks earlier. But whether it was two soulmates reuniting victoriously, or a simple chemical reaction in my brain, I knew I loved him, too. We made love for the second time that night, and it was just as wonderful as the first time.

Despite our instant connection, we managed to wait six months before moving in together. That had been fifteen years ago. And it had been a mostly wonderful fifteen years. We argued about once a year, and each time it was devastating, realizing we wouldn't always live in perfect harmony. But we also resolved our differences pretty quickly, too, and the arguments were more trivial each year. The past three years, we hadn't argued at all.

Well, once. When Justin told me he wanted to stop his chemotherapy and let Nature take its course, I argued. He'd won that one, though to be honest, it probably wouldn't have made much difference in any event. Pancreatic cancer wasn't that easy to combat. He'd died a little over four months ago. His last words were, "We're legally married. That means one day you can do proxy work in the temple and we'll be married forever."

"Honey, the Church isn't true," I whispered back.

"I want to be with you forever," he insisted. "Promise me you'll go to the temple once the Prophet has a revelation."

"I promise, Justin." Who wouldn't say anything to comfort a dying man?

"I love you, Fletcher."

"I love you, too."

Then he closed his eyes and died. Just like that. It didn't seem real. I felt like a participant on a reality show, when the "reality" was really scripted. Now the cameras were off, and it was time for Justin to quit playing his role of sick person. It was time for us to leave the hospital and go home.

I signed some papers donating Justin's body to the University of Utah medical school and then drove back to the house, looking at the autumn leaves falling from the trees along the road.

Thanksgiving had been difficult, and Christmas had been horrible, but today was Valentine's Day, and though this was a throwaway holiday for most people, it had always been one of Justin's favorites. I went to my closet and pulled out a shoebox full of cards. I had rubber bands around the Christmas ones, another around the birthday ones, and now I set down the batch of Valentine's Day cards.

The cards themselves were all different—a bunny looking longingly at another bunny, a cute dog holding a box of chocolates in his mouth, a handsome man holding a dove. But inside each card, the inscription was exactly the same: Fletcher, I know I must have been valiant in the Pre-existence, or Heavenly Father would not have rewarded me with you. I loved you then, I love you know, and I'll love you for the rest of eternity.

The only thing that was different from the first card and all those that followed were the additional words tagged on. "Still true."

I read each card in the stack, letting the words hit me over and over again as if each card said those words for the first time.

I wished I could make a movie called *Valentine's Day*, starring Joseph Gordon-Levitt, where the lovers get to meet again for the first time in an endless loop. When he was young, Justin had looked just like the actor. "I'll look like that throughout eternity," he'd reminded me every year on his birthday.

"And I'll keep looking like Jonah Hill," I pointed out.

"That'll all be taken care of in the Resurrection." The last time he'd said it, he'd paused and then added, "I always see you now the way you'll look then."

I was forty-three and had never been much of a looker. I knew I was never going to find another husband, given the material I had to work with. But the prospect of another forty years alone was pretty daunting. I needed to go out tonight and be with people. Though only couples would go out on a night like this, so that would probably be the worst move I could make.

I looked up movies online. *Fifty Shades of Grey* was playing. Neither Justin nor I had ever been anything but vanilla.

But our vanilla sex had kept us both interested right up till the end. Or at least till near the end. Justin had finally lost all interest in sex his last month, apologizing to me as if I cared. "That's the least of my worries," I assured him.

"I don't want us to ever lose our flame," he said.

"You'll get your flame back when you go into remission."

He shook his head. "Don't talk like that. Be honest with me."

"You'll get your flame back when you get resurrected." It was no more honest, but he accepted that one.

So what else was playing tonight? I browsed the theater website and saw my other options. There was *American Sniper*. It sounded terrible, though when I watched the news earlier today and learned that Isis had burned to death forty-five prisoners, I had to wonder where all this hatred was going to end up.

I didn't want to think about hate on Valentine's Day.

Birdman was also playing, and it was doing well in the awards circles, so it would probably be worth seeing. It sounded too serious for my mood today, though.

Then there was *The Imitation Game*. That sounded serious as well, of course, about the tragic life of the gay English codebreaker from World War II. And I'd read about biographical issues with the film as well. While Turing was depicted as gay, his actual sexual relationships were glossed over in favor of one with a platonic female friend. Still, the movie looked like my best option for the evening. I could call some of my friends, but the six people I knew were all part of three couples and would have plans of their own.

I'd lost twenty pounds during Justin's illness and thought briefly about gorging myself on vanilla ice cream tonight. Maybe I could eat myself to death over the next few years. At that point, either I'd be reunited with Justin as he predicted, or I'd cease to exist and wouldn't be conscious of my loneliness any longer.

But it wasn't exactly loneliness that I was feeling, I realized. I did have friends. And I had my work. I had my volunteer activities. I had my hobbies. My life wasn't empty. It was simply that I missed my husband.

"Please, Heavenly Father," I prayed. "Be real. Can you do that for me? Be real and take care of Justin."

I shook my head and stood up. I grabbed a sip of water from the kitchen and then headed for the door. *The Imitation Game* started in forty-five minutes. Plenty of time to get there, but I preferred waiting in the lobby over going crazy at home.

Just as I reached for the door handle, the doorbell rang. I jumped and put my hand on my heart. Peeking through the peephole, I saw a young man with a cap. I opened the door.

"Fletcher Stevens?" he asked.

"Yes?"

He handed me a bouquet of yellow daffodils, orange alstroemeria, and purple iris. The very flowers Justin used to give me every Valentine's Day. I looked at the young man in confusion as he pointed out the card attached to the bouquet.

"Who sent this?" I asked.

"Don't know," he replied. "I just deliver." He stood there a moment longer, until I realized he was waiting for a tip. I handed him the three ones I had left in my wallet. He didn't look very impressed but nodded and left. I realized I'd probably been insensitive. He was out working instead of spending time with his beloved. I should have been more generous. Justin would have been generous.

I opened the card. "Fletcher, I know I must have been valiant in the Pre-existence, or Heavenly Father would not have rewarded me with you. I loved you then, I love you know, and I'll love you for the rest of eternity."

Oh, my god.

Then I saw the two words scribbled on the back of the card. "Still true." It was all in Justin's handwriting.

Had my husband put one of our friends up to this? Written this card ahead of time, knowing this first Valentine's Day without him would be so difficult? I went to my contact list and punched Kirby's number.

"Nope, that wasn't us," he said. "But that was sure sweet of Justin to do."

I called Paul.

He laughed. "That sure sounds like Justin. But no, that wasn't us."

Finally, I called Hartley. He denied any participation either.

I looked at my watch. I didn't want to miss the movie, but I couldn't take my eyes away from the flowers and the card. I saw the phone number for the florist and dialed that next. I explained who I was and what had just happened.

"Oh, that," said the woman on the other end of the phone. "Yes, I remember perfectly. Your husband came in and set up a special account. He handed us a stack of signed cards and arranged to have us deliver a bouquet to you every Valentine's Day for the next thirty years."

"Th-thirty years?" I asked.

"Assuming we're still in business by then." She laughed.

I hung up the phone and sat down on my sofa with a heavy plop. I wanted to cry, but I was too happy. I suddenly wanted to lose more weight so I'd be around for another thirty years. Of course, what would happen the first Valentine's Day after I turned seventy-three? Did I need to time my death that carefully? I smiled. It was just like Justin. He'd always loved that scene from *The Wizard of Oz* where the Wicked Witch shakes the hourglass at Dorothy. "Fletcher, you've got just thirty years till that hourglass runs empty. Then I'll have you, my pretty."

I went over to the vase where I'd put the flowers, and I sniffed the daffodils. They had such a wonderful, earthy smell. My favorite.

I looked at my watch. I'd probably miss the previews, but I could still make it in time for the movie itself.

The Imitation Game. What I wanted to see was *Valentine's Day* with Joseph Gordon-Levitt.

"Please, Heavenly Father," I prayed, "let the Church still be true. Let us have an eternal marriage. Let me be with my husband again." I opened the door but then looked back inside, up toward the ceiling. "Please."

I walked outside and climbed into the car.

Teacher of the Millennium

The results would be announced soon. The past three years, I'd come in second, third, and second again for the school's Teacher of the Year award. I only had two more years until I retired, and I desperately wanted this recognition for my thirty-five years of hard work. While I'd always been a decent teacher, I'd increased my efforts by double these past few years. Other teachers petered out as they neared retirement, but I wanted to know that all the misery had been worth the effort, that I'd made a difference in the world, even if it was just teaching literature to students who would never pick up another book once they graduated.

"Steven, Nancy, and Craig," I said, addressing three of the seniors in my class, "your group will present *To Kill a Mockingbird* next." I tried to flatten a small wrinkle on my bosom. "Everybody ready?"

The three students nodded in resignation and trudged to the front of the class. I knew that different students learned in different ways, and even a single student benefitted from different approaches to learning. So I gave oral lectures, presented visual slides, assigned respectable readings, created social learning environments with group projects, forced a certain level of performance by regular testing, and gave my students opportunities to speak in front of others. Both the preparation to speak and the fear of judgment spurred students to a higher level. It was kind of like the bishop asking teenagers to speak in Sacrament meeting, or calling young adults to perform as missionaries, or requiring all members to read the scriptures daily, and listen to General Conference talks, and write in their journals. The Church knew that to become good, knowledgeable, committed Mormons, the members needed to learn in a variety of ways.

"I want to talk about a scene from the book that isn't in the movie," Nancy began. "It's the scene where Miss Maudie's house burns. The neighbors help her save her furniture, but she loses the house. But she's very cheerful about the whole thing, saying she wanted a smaller house anyway. And the fire gives Boo Radley a chance to put a blanket on Scout to protect her from the cold winter night." Nancy stepped back, seeming relieved to be finished with her portion in twenty seconds. But I thought she could say more.

"I see," I said, "so Nancy, tell us what all that means."

Nancy looked very unhappy.

The girl wasn't going to make the leap and actually learn anything until she was forced to. It was the way Heavenly Father worked, too. As a teacher, and as a candidate for Teacher of the Year, I thought about these things often. None of us wanted all the trials of Earth life, but we accepted them in the Pre-Existence because we knew coming here was the only way to learn. It was a lot like Nancy signing up for this class, knowing at the outset she was going to complete the course having learned something. But like Nancy, all of us on the Earth probably didn't fully understand that simply coming to the Earth, or coming to English class, was enough to do the trick. Learning itself took work.

I hoped to be able to give a long talk about all this at Sacrament meeting soon. Or maybe at stake conference. That would be even better. Learning was hard, but learning how to help others learn was even harder. This must be how Heavenly Father felt most of the time. "Come on, Susan," he must be whispering to me every day, "you have to *do* something now in order to fully learn your lesson." No one liked the actual learning of the lesson, but everyone liked having learned it.

Nancy struggled with her interpretation, and I kept pushing for the next several minutes. When she finally looked like she was about to cry, I let up and asked Steven to present his piece.

But would Heavenly Father have let up, I wondered? Should I have kept pushing? I'd pushed more than ever this year, wanting that award. I could only get it if my students truly excelled. Maybe I'd ask Nancy another question after Steven finished.

Steven talked about the alleged rape, and how it was misogynistic to call Mayella a liar. "The author is trying to show racial injustice, but she ends up promoting gender injustice instead." He went on for a few more minutes, and while I didn't agree with everything he said, he was at least making conclusions and backing them up with details, something Nancy had been unable to do.

It made me think about racial inequality, and sexism, and poverty, and rape. A lesser person would wonder why Heavenly Father felt we needed to experience these things in order to learn about humanity to its fullest degree. If one needed to be raped in order to understand rape, what did that say about all the people who were never raped? Did they not learn everything they needed to know about humanity?

It was basically what Brother Maxwell had said in Gospel Doctrine class, shortly before he was excommunicated, so I knew it was preposterous. "If God is the most intelligent being in the universe," he'd said, "if he knows absolutely everything there is to know, why is it that he needs to create a learning system where we come to Earth to face such evil? Is facing evil the only way to learn?" Not very articulate, I'd thought at the time, planning on giving him a critique after class, but his comments had still struck a chord, since I'd been wondering how to finally achieve Teacher of the Year and the topic of learning was always on my mind. He went on in his pompous way, "God makes us suffer hunger and sexual abuse and ALS and car bombs and homelessness and concentration camps, all because he is so generous that he wants us to learn and grow. He is all-knowing, and this is the best he can do? In all his wisdom, he can't come up with a better way to teach?" While Brother Maxwell was criticizing, I was having an epiphany—those methods actually worked.

"So, Steven," I said, "do you think racism trumps sexism? Do you think sexism trumps racism?"

Steven looked at Nancy, who rolled her eyes, and then he looked back at me. "I think it's wrong to place these things in any kind of hierarchical order," he said. "It's truth that always matters. And justice."

Not bad. It *did* pay to push. "How do we know what's true," I said, "when what we are willing to believe is based so much on our pre-conceived ideas?" Steven looked at both Nancy and Craig before taking a deep breath and trying to answer. I could see a few beads of sweat forming on his forehead. He went on for another couple of minutes, and finally, it was Craig's turn to speak. He discussed the rabid dog scene, explaining that it wasn't enough for Atticus to be a moral hero. He had to be a physical hero as well. I let him talk.

These kids hated me sometimes. Several of them had left nasty notes on my desk recently. But I knew I was like the drill sergeant who finally turns a boy into a man. Heavenly Father was like that, too. So many people cursed God, but God was doing them a favor every day of their lives. It was like those children born without any pain receptors. They chewed off their fingertips, broke their bones, and generally led very short lives. Pain was an essential part of learning. Heavenly Father knew that and took advantage of that fact.

Sometimes, though, it seemed Heavenly Father chose to trigger every pain receptor in our body at the same time. It seemed he was giving us shingles when all we needed was a paper cut. But who was I to question the Supreme Teacher? I always wondered if I should be even harder on my students.

I thought of last night's news, when I learned that ISIS had burned over 100,000 books in Iraq, including priceless old manuscripts, something that cut a literature teacher to the core.

Could one learn from someone refusing to allow other people to learn?

If Heavenly Father permitted this pain to be inflicted, though, it must by definition be for our good, like all the other pain he inflicted.

So it made me wonder if we even needed books in the first place. In a sense, they were like life. Without a conflict, a story had no purpose. Without that same conflict, neither did a life.

At the same time, could there really be conflict if one had certitude? Mormons might experience misery at times, but that wasn't the same as conflict. Did Heavenly Father really need our help in supporting his instruction by having us teach pain by proxy through storytelling? Perhaps it was no great loss if all those books were gone. And maybe it was simply a waste of my life to have taught literature for thirty-five years, if literature showed conflict that didn't truly exist for people who had the truth.

Waste or not, I wanted that award.

As Craig continued speaking about heroism in a low, monotone voice, Brother Maxwell's rant came back to my mind. "God's plan is a failure because if having your leg blown off by a land mine is the only way to understand what it's like to have your leg blown off, not everyone learns that lesson. That means we don't all learn everything. And if it's okay for this person not to learn by suffering every horror, why is it okay to force that person to learn from it?" He'd paused, and one of the others in the Gospel Doctrine class left the room to get the bishop. Then he went on, "And if God didn't create a world where there were muggings and home invasions and workplace shooters in the first place, why would I *need* to learn about muggings and home invasions and workplace shootings?" He looked about the classroom, where most of the other adults were looking down at the scriptures in their laps. But I looked right back at Brother Maxwell. "The system sucks because God sucks." Then he shook his head. "Or let me put it another way. No loving god would invent such a system. If the ability to learn from misery is supposed to make me believe in God, it's not working."

The bishop and his first counselor came into the room a moment later and escorted Brother Maxwell out. We never knew the particulars, but a couple of weeks later, it was announced in Sacrament meeting that Brother Maxwell had been excommunicated.

Obviously something he needed to experience in order to learn.

That's why Church tribunals were called "courts of love." What some saw as punishment, the righteous realized was love. Any suffering the Lord inflicted upon us was done because he loved us so deeply. If *I* had to take courses in how to teach, didn't people realize that Heavenly Father had taken even more? Who could question someone who had earned fifty graduate degrees? A hundred? A thousand?

"How do you see Atticus as a physical hero," I asked Craig, "when he lets Mr. Ewell spit in his face without doing anything about it?"

Craig's confidence immediately sank out of him. He looked at me in confusion for a moment and then shrugged.

"You have to answer the question," I said. I thought that if pressed he might mention how Atticus had risked his life to stand guard at the jail.

"There *is* a hierarchy of heroism," Nancy cut in, though I could see her hand quivering. "Being a moral hero is better than being a physical hero. While Atticus is both, his moral heroism is greater than his physical heroism. So when he doesn't fight back physically, he is showing he is greater than Mr. Ewell."

Nancy looked afraid I might question her further, but I nodded and let the three students go back to their seats, which they took as quickly as possible. I'd gotten her to push herself, and that was even better than my pushing her. I really was a great teacher. I was sure to get that award this year.

I saw Principal Matthews stand up in the back of the class. I'd been so focused on the presentation I hadn't even seen him come in. He'd witnessed the entire scene. What a stroke of fortune. I knew I had to undergo observation before the winner of the award was announced. After today's class, I was a shoo-in for sure.

The principal motioned me over and I walked up to him confidently. He whispered, "See me during your free period," and then left the room.

It would be one of my interviews for the award. Every teacher up for it had to pass an interview with the principal first. This proved I was likely going to be a finalist in any event.

But finalist wasn't good enough. I wanted to win that award. If I did, I might even retire a year early, go out on a high note.

I wondered if I should assign a didactic reading next, perhaps *Pilgrim's Progress* or *Brideshead Revisited* or *Atlas Shrugged*. Sometimes students weren't up to reading a more nuanced text like Harper Lee's. But then, I wanted the experience to be hard. Maybe I'd assign *Moby Dick*. I frowned at the thought. Even I didn't fully understand *Moby Dick*. But challenging myself would be good, too.

The rest of the class proceeded nicely, as did the following ones, and two hours later, I was in Principal Matthews' office. "You wanted to see me, sir?"

"That was an impressive performance earlier," he said. "You certainly must know that you have both admirers and haters. We get emails about you every day. But I have to say, your students consistently do well on their exams. If you had to sum up your teaching theory in just a few words, what would you say is your main philosophy?"

I smiled at the easy question. "I believe in torture," I said simply. It was the way the Lord worked, the way the Church worked, too. Who could say that Visiting Teaching and Home Teaching weren't torture? God's teaching method was why being a Mormon was so often miserable. We might not have true conflict once we knew the truth, but there was certainly misery. My brother had killed himself after a year of electroshock therapy at Brigham Young University, but that was only because he was lazy and refused to learn how to be straight. It was unfortunate, but Heavenly Father couldn't *make* a person learn. He could only offer opportunities. I had suffered through thirty-five years of whiny, listless students, but I had led several on to greatness. Four of my students had gone on to earn PhD's in English literature. Two had become attorneys. Three had become doctors. Every one of those students still wrote me.

Nine out of what? Four or five thousand? I understood now how Heavenly Father felt allowing the elect into the Celestial Kingdom, and the idea made me smile. All this misery *had* taught me something. I knew it would.

"Torture?" said Principal Matthews uncertainly.

"You have to push someone so hard that they're miserable," I said. "You can only truly learn when you're miserable." I thought about my early years and added, "I miss the days when we could paddle students, but you can inflict pain without a paddle, too."

"I see." The principal looked at me another moment, flipped through some papers on his desk, and then looked back up at me again. After adjusting his tie, he stood up and offered his hand. "Well, I appreciate you coming in to talk to me, Susan." I smiled, shook his hand, and left the office.

I was going to be Teacher of the Year. And one day, when I became a god, I'd be Teacher of the Millennium, Teacher of the Eternities, inflicting misery on billions of my spirit children. Because I loved them.

I walked back to my classroom and started grading papers during the rest of my free period. I got out my red pen and began to write.

Sealed with a Kiss

"Will you marry me, Breanne?" I asked. I was hanging from a tree branch by my knees, upside down. I dug a tiny box out of my jeans pocket and opened it, the blood pounding in my head. Breanne's face was upside down to me, as she was standing beside the tree, so I couldn't gauge her reaction.

She kissed me and said, "Yes, Grant, I'll marry you."

I grabbed the branch with my hands and flipped my way out of the tree. "I'll do everything I can to make you happy," I promised. I took the ring out of the box and slipped it onto her finger.

"You already do." She wiggled her left hand so I could see the tiny diamond reflecting in the late afternoon sun. "This is almost as nice as the ginger snap cookies you baked for me last week."

"Almost?" I asked.

"Well, maybe a *little* better." She had beautiful dimples when she smiled.

I took her hands and smiled in return. "So I can baptize you this Sunday?" I pressed.

She looked down at the grass for a moment and then back at me. "Yes, you can baptize me," she said.

Breanne had been raised in a Presbyterian home but her family hadn't attended services in years. As a young adult, Breanne had never bothered about religion. Until she met me at the Puyallup Fair. We both lived in Seattle, and after our third date, I asked her to start attending Sacrament meeting with me. I didn't suggest the entire three-hour block, of course, as I didn't want to scare her off. As our relationship progressed over the next four months, I finally asked her to take the missionary lessons. She did so half-heartedly. She didn't dislike Mormonism; she simply felt indifferent to religion. Since I knew I could never marry outside the Church, I fasted quite a lot during those months. We also watched several LDS movies on DVD. We drove past the temple in Bellevue. I invited her to Family Home Evening with my parents and younger brother who still lived at home. I gave her some Deseret Book love stories to read.

And now she'd agreed to be baptized! And to marry me! Life couldn't get any better than this.

The day of the baptism, I was probably more nervous than Breanne was. She'd declined the white jumpsuit the ward offered her, wearing instead her own pair of white cotton dress pants and a long-sleeved white shirt. She didn't have a slip, but she bought a white T-shirt to wear under her shirt, in addition to her white bra and panties. "Should I repaint my toenails?" she asked before we left for the church. They were currently colored a bright blue.

"I think you're okay as long as all your clothes are white," I returned.

"But after I dry off, I get to wear regular clothes, right?"

"A nice dress." I'd explained all of this to her already.

"You do realize," she said, "that we're going to have to wear these baptismal outfits again sometime after we're married. As a prelude to Date Night sex." She smiled her signature smile, and I turned red. I enjoyed how much freer she was in talking about these things than I was. I hoped her attitude would rub off on me after we married. We had already begun discussing different sexual acts, to see if we thought we wanted the same thing. Breanne had already experienced sex, of course, and I listened to her views a little enviously.

Of course, with her baptism today, all those offenses would be washed away. And after we were married, sex would no longer be a sin. To be honest, I loved her so much, I really couldn't quite believe sex with Breanne even before marriage would be a terrible thing. How could it be?

But I didn't want to louse up any chance we had of marrying in the temple a year after she joined the Church. Being sealed, really. We'd marry civilly well before then. I was still torn between marrying in the temple exactly a year after our civil marriage, so I wouldn't have to remember more than one anniversary, or marrying a year after Breanne was baptized, which would probably be about nine months after our civil wedding. I'd discuss it with my bishop so that I made the right decision.

Today's focus was on the baptism itself, the beginning of our path to the Celestial Kingdom together. I'd only baptized three people on my mission to France, and here I was baptizing another soul, a full 33% of my mission total, just because I'd ordered a hot dog at the Puyallup Fair.

The Lord worked in mysterious ways.

I remembered Breanne smiling at me at the fair, a little brazenly, and then opening her mouth wide to engulf her hot dog.

Heavenly Father was sure to send us countless blessings after our wedding for having resisted the urges so many others our age fell victim to.

In the font, I took hold of Breanne in the authorized baptismal manner, raised my arm to the square, and dipped her completely below the surface of the water. Not even a fingertip could remain above the surface or the baptism would have to be redone. I felt a cascade of love flowing through my heart as I realized I was giving my beloved such a wonderful gift. I lifted her back up out of the water, and there was suddenly an audible gasp from everyone seated in the observation room.

Breanne had forgotten to wear both her T-shirt and her bra underneath her white shirt. Her dark nipples were clearly visible to me, to my parents, to my brother, to the bishop, and to everyone else in attendance.

Breanne leaned forward and whispered in my ear. "I just wanted today to be as memorable for you as it is for me." Then she started climbing out of the font toward the women's dressing room. My problem was that while I myself was quite covered, the wet clothing was still rather form-fitting, creating an awkward situation as I tried to exit toward the men's room without anyone noticing the effect Breanne had had on me.

My father gave Breanne the gift of the Holy Ghost, and then we all went back to my parents' house for dinner.

"Guess what?" Breanne asked me after services the following Sunday. She was now attending for the full three hours.

"You finished the Book of Mormon?" I asked.

She shook her head. "Still in 2 Nephi," she replied. "But the bishop called me to teach Primary."

"Already? Don't you need to attend Sunday School and Relief Society yourself for a while to get up to speed?"

"Bishop Alford said teaching ten-year-olds would force me to study."

I shrugged. "Well, he's inspired to make these kinds of decisions. Are you going to accept?"

"I already did. And I promised to read at least four more pages of the Book of Mormon tonight."

"I have it all on CD if you prefer."

"No, no, I'm good. Thanks."

"Have you been praying about where we should go on our honeymoon?" I asked. I was kind of hoping for Salt Lake or Nauvoo or Palmyra.

"I have a strong burning in my bosom when I think of Hawaii."

I felt my eyebrows rising in surprise and tried to appear casual. "Well, there's a lovely temple there. It'll probably be too soon for you to do baptisms for the dead, but we can still stroll around the grounds and take pictures."

"I hear the beaches are nice, too."

"Have you bought your one-piece yet?"

She nodded. "Bright red." She saw my expression and went on. "People will be looking at the loud color instead of at me."

That made sense.

We sang a lot of hymns together during the next few months as the wedding approached. We'd start kissing, would kiss a little more, and then our lips would start to wander a little away from the face. Sometimes it would be me, and sometimes it would be Breanne, but at some point, one of us would stop kissing and start singing, "Come, come, ye saints," and after a few minutes, we'd give each other one last peck, and I'd head back to my apartment for a cold shower.

The wedding itself was nominal, held in my parents' living room, with only a few guests. The good part of not being able to marry in the temple yet was that Breanne's family was able to attend. My own parents would be present when we would be sealed later, but Breanne's parents wouldn't be allowed in the temple, even though they didn't smoke or drink. Of course, even if they'd been regular churchgoers and paid tithing to their own church, it still wouldn't do them any good. One had to follow the right religion to be worthy to enter the temple.

"This is such a long flight," Breanne whispered later, a few hours after the plane took off for Honolulu. The first movie had finished a few minutes earlier, and the flight attendants had just picked up the cans and other trash on one of their sweeps through the cabin. "I'm not sure I can wait till we get to the hotel."

I laughed. "Well, there aren't many options around that," I pointed out.

"There's one." She raised an eyebrow and motioned toward the back of the plane.

Was she suggesting we make out in the back row? I'd noticed when we boarded that every seat was taken.

"The lavatory, dummy," she said. "We can start our marriage as members of the Mile High Club."

"The Mile High Club?"

"Good grief, Grant. Just follow me." She stood up and made her way to the bathroom. After a moment, I followed, waiting outside the door.

Three minutes later, there were two other people behind me in line. Another minute after that, Breanne opened the door and peeked out. She shook her head, grabbed my hand, and led me back to our seats.

Things were different in the hotel. I took a shower, brushed my teeth, flossed, and rinsed with mouthwash. I left the bathroom without my garments on, wearing only a robe. I stopped dead in my tracks when I saw the bed. Breanne was lying splayed out on top of the covers in the shape of an X. I had never seen a naked woman before. My eyes were drawn immediately to her crotch, but instead of the pubic hair and who knows what else I expected to see, I saw instead something foamy and white.

What the—

"After you lick off all the whipped cream, we can discuss what you'll need to do next."

Suddenly, I felt very sinful. I'd been anticipating the day when we could finally have sex without it being wicked, but since we still weren't married in the temple, the marriage didn't quite feel legitimate. All of this still felt like a transgression. "Does sex count if we're not *really* married?" I asked out loud.

"Come here, fella," said Breanne. "I'll make it count."

What I'd meant, of course, was did it count as a sin. Breanne's confirmation hardly put my mind at ease. And yet, it only took me a few minutes before I was fully in the mood and participating in every way I could think of.

Breanne taught me a few new ways to think of it.

By the end of our three-day honeymoon, I felt like a pro. I understood now the swagger of some of the other men in my office. What was great was that even over the next few months, Breanne managed to keep things fresh and new every night. And I mean every night. But what was also surprising was that while sex seemed to be a bigger part of our relationship than the Church, Breanne truly did seem to be responding to the Spirit every day.

Each day brought a new discovery. "Guess what I learned?" was one of the first things she said to me after I came home from work every evening. Breanne had balked at first at giving up her job, but we were trying to get pregnant right away, and I wanted her to feel at home as a housewife before she was forced to stay home as a mother.

"I learned that Mormons were massacred at Haun's Mill."

"I learned that a lot of people died on the trek across the plains."

"I learned that a whole riverboat full of Mormons blew up on the Missouri River."

"I learned that seagulls ate all the crickets that were destroying the first crop in Salt Lake."

"I learned that Parley P. Pratt escaped jail by tricking the dog that was sent to chase him."

I always enjoyed hearing the things Breanne was learning. She was taking everything a little more seriously every day. It was like watching a rose blossom before my eyes.

"Guess what I learned?" she said again today after I returned from a hard day at work. We'd been married three months and were still celebrating each month as a mini-anniversary.

I looked at her expectantly, waiting to hear her latest discovery. Something about Jackson County, Missouri? Something about Kirtland?

"I learned that I'm pregnant," she said simply.

I dropped my satchel on the floor and rushed to her. "Honey, what wonderful news!"

"Our first baby god," said Breanne.

I laughed, but then I paused. If she miscarried before we were sealed in the temple, we might lose this baby forever. It had been six months since Breanne was baptized, so we were still a good half year away from a trip to the temple in Bellevue.

"You're frowning," said Breanne. "Will you still be attracted to me while I'm pregnant? Can we still have sex?"

"You could never stop being sexy," I replied, and I proved it there on the living room sofa. I had discovered that chocolate syrup on a certain body part of my own also led to some exciting times, especially when followed with strawberry jam on certain parts of Breanne's body.

We kept special sex sheets ready to throw over whatever surface we planned to use on a given day.

Her new friends from the ward held a baby shower for Breanne. I didn't make enough money for a larger home just yet, but we already had two bedrooms, so we'd be okay for a couple of years. We spent the next few Saturdays roaming yard sales to pick up baby clothes in a variety of sizes. "We're not going to give our baby a million toys," I said, "and clutter up the house and spoil our child. Just a few really nice toys and that's all."

"How about this cute stuffed red panda?" suggested Breanne at one yard sale.

"It looks like a fox."

"It's a panda."

"It's far too big. Let's get the baby something he can cuddle with once he's a toddler."

"Once *she* is, you mean." We'd decided not to find out the sex of the baby until it was born, even if that did cause certain problems with the preparation. You couldn't buy everything yellow. And pink just wouldn't do for a boy, but girls could wear blue. "I want the red panda," Breanne insisted. "If the baby doesn't like it, I'll keep it."

Hormones, I thought. But I went ahead and bought the stuffed animal.

She positioned the toy so that it was staring at us as we had sex that night. The exhibitionism was a little titillating.

I kept returning home from work to hear Breanne's excited comments. "Guess what I learned today?" I always smiled happily at the words.

"I learned that the Church supported women's suffrage."

"I learned that the Tabernacle was built without a single nail."

"I learned that the Prophet was inspired to create elevator shafts in the Salt Lake temple, even before elevators were invented."

It was almost like already having a child, watching the enthusiasm for learning in my beautiful wife.

On the evening of our fifth mini-anniversary, Breanne greeted me at the door again. "Guess what I learned today?"

I smiled, anxious to hear what new faith-promoting fact Breanne had picked up.

"I learned that I have cervical cancer."

I stared at her. Was that supposed to be a joke?

"And I'm not taking chemotherapy. It'll kill the baby. I'm going to try to live long enough to have her first."

I kept staring for a long moment, and then I rushed over and held her tight. Of course, we talked about treatment anyway, but she was adamant. She was already approximately four months pregnant, and the doctor had given her roughly six months to live. She should be able to have the baby, and then, if there was still any hope, she could begin treatment at that time.

We'd barely have time to get sealed in the temple, making the one-year mark near the end of her pregnancy and near the end of her prognosis. I decided to talk to the stake president the following Sunday. I met with him in his office at the stake center, explained how Breanne was learning more and more about the Church every day, that she had now almost finished the Book of Mormon. Of course, I was fudging a little on that last part, since she had really only reached the middle of the book. But I explained truthfully that Breanne had never missed a Sunday, was fasting once a month, and why we needed to be able to marry before the official one-year anniversary of her baptism. "Even ten months would do," I said. "It's not only a matter of our own sealing, but the truth is, she's likely to lose the baby, and we can't get sealed later to a fetus. We want this spirit sealed to us regardless of what happens. Is there any way you can make an exception and let us marry a little early?"

President Webb looked at me for a long moment and then nodded slightly. "I'll think about it, and pray about it, and confer with my counselors. You certainly make a strong case, and it's only a minor exception. But I can't guarantee anything just yet. Come back and see me next Sunday."

Breanne and I went to the temple on our seventh mini-anniversary. Because her parents couldn't attend, I asked my own parents to abstain as well. Given the grim nature of the ceremony, it didn't feel as celebratory as I'd hoped in any event. Breanne was taking pain medication and had to be prompted several times during her endowment session before she got the words right. I hoped everything counted up in heaven.

When we kissed over the altar, though, I felt a blanket of peace descend upon me. It was done. We were sealed. We would be husband and wife throughout the eternities. We would become gods in the Celestial Kingdom together.

I started to cry.

"It'll be okay, Grant," Breanne whispered. "It'll be okay."

Walking slowly back out to the car, Breanne surprised me. "We need to have a little mini-honeymoon now."

"But we can't even have sex anymore. It hurts you too much."

"There are still some things we can do," she said, smiling weakly. After I climbed behind the steering wheel, Breanne unzipped my pants in the temple parking lot and went down on me. After I came, she flung open her car door and threw up on the asphalt. We were both crying as I pulled out of the lot and headed for home.

A month later, we celebrated two mini-anniversaries, eight months of our civil wedding and one month of our temple wedding. Breanne was getting weaker and weaker. It seemed unlikely she'd last the six months the doctor had hoped. I wasn't sure she'd even make it anywhere near term. The baby still seemed healthy, though, so we tried whatever we could. I read three books about cancer diets and cooked a different meal every night, hoping to find one that Breanne could tolerate.

"Guess what I learned today?"

"What's that, honey?"

"I learned you'll get married in the temple to someone else after I die, and we'll practice polygamy in the Celestial Kingdom for eternity." She didn't look happy at the discovery.

"I'll never marry anyone else in the temple," I promised.

"Oh, Grant, then none of your other children will be sealed to you. You can't do that."

I felt as unhappy now as she looked. I hugged her and wondered why Heavenly Father was punishing us like this. "I have HPV now, too," I whispered. "Maybe I'll get cancer myself and join you soon." I wasn't even sure if the virus caused cancer in men.

"Well, I certainly don't want that, either," said Breanne. "You need to stay to raise the baby." She paused and then added, "It's a girl, just as I'd hoped. I couldn't bear waiting when...when I might not be around long enough to find out naturally."

"A girl," I breathed. "How wonderful. I'll raise her to be just like you."

An hour later, the phone rang. It was President Webb. "Grant, I need to see you. It's pretty urgent. Can you come down to the stake center tonight?"

After I finished preparing dinner for Breanne, I drove on over and met the president in his office. "What is it?" I asked. Had my father committed some grave sin and was facing excommunication? Had my brother? Steven had just submitted his mission papers. Was there some problem with his application? The president had sounded serious over the phone, but he certainly couldn't be calling me to any important position at this point in Breanne's illness.

"Grant," said President Webb after shaking my hand and motioning for me to sit down, "I'm afraid there's bad news."

I looked at him expectantly.

"Salt Lake has informed me that I overstepped my authority when I gave Breanne a temple recommend. They say she has to wait the full year before she can go to the temple. The Lord's house is a house of order. We have to follow the rules. They're going to invalidate your temple marriage."

My mouth fell open.

"It's not long now," the president went on. "Only another month. You can get married then."

"President," I said slowly, "my wife is over seven months pregnant, and she weighs 115 pounds. Even if she's still alive in one month, she'll be in no condition to go to the temple."

"You can always marry her by proxy," he countered softly. "And the baby is already far enough along to survive her death. You can be sealed to him later."

"Her," I corrected.

The stake president nodded.

"Is there anyone I can talk to?" I asked. "One of the apostles?"

"The decision has already been made," he answered. "In fact, the marriage has already been canceled."

I stared at him.

"Perhaps you had better not tell your wife."

I stood up, and the president did as well. He offered his hand, but I didn't take it. "You can go to hell," I said and walked out the door.

I drove around for a half hour before heading back to the house. I needed more time than that, but I didn't want to leave Breanne alone for too long. She was lying on the sofa when I returned. She looked up at me and smiled weakly.

"Guess what I learned today?" I said teasingly.

"What?"

"The stake president called me to be the new bishop," I said, "but I won't start the job for a few more months yet."

"How will you take care of the baby?"

I'd felt telling her some good news would help her, but I clearly hadn't thought it out. "The ward is going to have the Relief Society take turns babysitting," I invented on the spot.

"Oh, that's good," Breanne said softly. "I'm so worried about you."

I kneeled beside her and kissed her gently on the lips.

Two weeks later, at Breanne's doctor appointment at the hospital, the doctor pulled me aside. "We're going to have to do a C-section and take the baby today. It's getting weaker, too, and won't make it if we try to go to term."

"Okay," I said.

"You have to understand," she went on, "your wife is not likely to survive the surgery."

I nodded, blinking. "Does she know?"

"She knows." The doctor paused. "And I can't guarantee the baby will survive, either."

I went in to see Breanne before they wheeled her away. I held her hand and smiled. "You're going to be a mommy," I said. I squeezed her fingers.

"Guess what I learned today?" Breanne's voice was almost too soft to hear.

"What?"

"I learned that loving you makes everything okay." She smiled and shook her head. "I'm sorry. I lied. The truth is I learned that a long time ago." I leaned down and kissed her on the lips.

I followed the doctor, put on my gown and mask, and entered the delivery room to watch as one life ended and another began. They didn't let me hold the baby, rushing her off to an incubator instead. Almost seven and a half months, but far underweight. When I turned back to look at Breanne, the nurse was shaking his head.

I sat outside the nursery the rest of the afternoon and all night, afraid to leave the hospital. My parents came to sit with me for a while, and I confided what the stake president had told me. "Son," said my father, putting his hand on my knee, "you committed no sin. You married in full faith, as honorable members of the Church. The Lord won't revoke your wedding because of what a few men said."

"Even if those men are apostles?"

"Apostles make mistakes, too."

"But what if?" I asked. "What if?"

"Son, you're a grown man. You're a husband. A father. A widower." He paused and patted my knee. "At some point you have to be mature enough to see the truth."

"The truth?" I asked weakly.

"What your father is trying to say," my mother interrupted, "is that you two would be sealed for eternity even if there were no Church." She smiled, her soft wrinkles promising wisdom.

I nodded, still unsure.

The baby died just before dawn. I hadn't even named her yet.

I drove home, called in sick to work, and picked up the Book of Mormon. I opened to the Book of Ether, which Breanne had just started, and began reading for her by proxy.

The Dinner Party

"Carmen! Drew! It's so good to see you!" Mom hugged us as we came through the door, making a fuss as if it hadn't just been a month ago when we'd all had dinner together the last time. She took our coats and threw them on the bed in the spare bedroom. My old bedroom when I was still attending the University of Utah, where I'd met Carmen while working on my Masters.

"Hi Amelia! Hi Gordon!" said Carmen in her thick accent, greeting my sister and her husband. Carmen was from Santiago but despite her accent spoke flawless English. She had a degree in English literature. My degrees were in business, of course. I had wanted to be a General Authority one day. Gordon was working on his PhD in Statistics. He'd never rise up in the hierarchy. Amelia was four months pregnant with their first child.

Dad came over and gave us a hug as well. Family was everything to Mormons. We all got together once a month so that we'd stay close even now that my sister and I were both married.

"Dinner's ready!" Mom announced only seconds later. Mom refused to let Carmen or Amelia contribute anything to the meal, wanting to prove to everyone she was still the ultimate authority in homemaking.

The ultimate authority.

I wasn't sure I believed in an ultimate authority anymore. Not my boss, not my bishop, not the Prophet. Not even God. But that was not the kind of thing one shared over a family dinner. I hadn't even shared it with Carmen yet.

My wife was asking why I kept using condoms, wondering why we didn't try to start a family of our own right away as we were supposed to do. I didn't give her the clear answer she deserved—that I wanted to figure out what I believed and determine if our marriage was going to survive a difference in religious conviction before I brought any kids into the equation.

Evenings like tonight made me want to stay in the fold. And also made me want to bolt once and for all.

"Your father had a wonderful experience at the temple this week," said Mom, setting down a plate of fried chicken on the table. "Tell them about it, Harold." She carried a huge dish of green bean casserole over from the oven.

"Let's wait till we're all sitting down," Dad replied. "Maureen, sit so we can say the blessing."

Mom giggled at her oversight and sat down on the edge of her seat, ready to jump up once the blessing had been offered. Dad didn't even ask if anyone else wanted to say the prayer. He automatically gave the blessing himself. "We thank thee for this bounty." "Please bless this food that it will be nutritious to us." "Please bless the hands that prepared it." Dad had given the same prayer thousands of times, but he said it each time as if it were all new. I watched him as he spoke now. He truly thought he was talking to someone real.

Was he? I wished I knew. Everyone else had the benefit of certainty. What a wonderful gift from God that must be.

How could that gift be from God if there was no God?

Was it a gift?

Soon we had all scooped spoonfuls of green beans with cream of mushroom soup and French-fried onions onto our plates. We added scalloped potatoes, baby English peas, and a piece of fried chicken as well. Mom always insisted we drink milk with dinner. Soft drinks were allowed at other meals, but only milk was acceptable in the evening.

"You never fail to please, Mom," I said. She beamed in response.

While I was basking in the love and the comfort food, I also felt a little detached. Mom spoke about her Visiting Teachers who'd come by this week with a special message about obedience. Amelia talked about a baby quilt she was designing and sewing. Carmen talked about the Sunday School lesson on faith she had given earlier today. Gordon talked about a book he was reading by President Monson on sacrifice. At least he wasn't talking about statistics. And Dad finally told us the story from the temple.

"So I'd been working at the veil all during my shift, and I finally finished and got to sit in the Celestial Room for a few minutes. I felt an incredible peace. I knew I'd helped some spirits on the Other Side who'd been waiting for years to have their endowments done. I saw the temple president on the far side of the room talking to another man dressed in white. I was curious because the man wasn't wearing the rest of the temple clothes, just the white."

"Honey, don't talk about temple clothes outside of the temple."

"I'm not talking about the clothes, Maureen. It's the man I'm talking about. So anyway, after this guy left, I walked over to the president and asked who he'd been talking to. And do you know what he said?"

Everyone shook their heads, their mouths full.

"He said, 'You saw him, Brother Broyles? That was Moroni. He likes to keep watch over his statues, and he let me know there was a problem with the one on the temple. But I'll take care of it right away.'"

"You saw the angel Moroni?" Amelia asked.

"Yes, he did," Mom answered for him. "Isn't that wonderful? He may be called to be the next temple president after this one leaves."

Everyone swallowed and stared at my father.

I didn't believe a word of it. Well, I believed the account as my father told it. I just didn't believe the temple president. It was like the witnesses to the Book of Mormon who didn't actually see the gold plates with their "physical" eyes. It was like the tingling I used to feel when I heard particularly good talks at church. I used to believe that was the Holy Ghost testifying to me. But I felt the same tingling when I saw movies like *Schindler's List* and *Norma Rae* and *The Miracle Worker*. Was the Lord testifying to me that Helen Keller really learned to spell "water"?

These family dinners were supposed to make me feel love, feel the oneness of being part of the gospel, one in our pursuit of the Celestial Kingdom.

"Did anyone else see him?" I asked. I wanted him to tell me something undeniable. We were taught we couldn't depend on another person's testimony, but relying on my father might get me through this rough patch.

"There was no one else in the room at the time. It was the end of the day."

"I thought those kinds of things only happened in the Holy of Holies," said Amelia, chewing on a chicken leg.

"The Celestial Room is the next best thing," Dad replied. "Especially at that time of evening. It's so peaceful."

"I love the Celestial Room," said Carmen. "The endowment ceremony can be a little long, but it's so wonderful once you get through the veil."

"It must be so nice working at the veil," said Gordon.

Dad nodded. "You get a sense of what it will be like getting into heaven. It's...it's a victorious feeling like nothing else I've ever experienced."

"Well, I'm sure working hard to get there," said Amelia with a smile. "Do you know how many mornings I've thrown up in the past few months?" Everyone laughed and put another spoonful of food in their mouths.

The conversation continued as we finished the meal, the talk drifting to the approach of Armageddon, obvious with the rise of militant Islam and the decay of America with Obama in charge and the threat of Hillary to follow. There was a calming unity of thought among Latter-day Saints almost anywhere I'd ever gone. I could attend church services in Salt Lake or Los Angeles or Atlanta or even Naples or Paris, and I would feel completely at home. Only I didn't feel at home even in Salt Lake anymore. I felt like I did every time I was asked to sustain a local member for a new leadership calling. Everyone in the room always raised their right hand in full support. It was unheard of to go against the flow. Then it would be announced triumphantly, "The vote was unanimous." But was everyone else just raising their hand for the same reason I was? Just so we wouldn't cause a fuss? I wondered if the avoidance of serious debate was really the highest good for which one could aim.

Was unhappy discord really a loftier goal? I saw Amelia absentmindedly rubbing her stomach and tried to be happy for her. I watched Carmen's adoring eyes following my mother and smiled.

As Mom set plates of apple pie in front of each of us, Dad spoke up again. "If you could invite anyone at all over for dinner, who would it be?"

Now I felt I was back in Single Adult Family Home Evening, playing Truth or Dare. Was there a Church handbook out there prescribing acceptable dinner topics for families? Perhaps it was kept secret until we had our first child. In recent months, we'd discussed "What would you do if you had to rely on your food storage and your neighbor hadn't prepared?" and "How do you think the Lord will arrange to have his temple built in Jerusalem?" and "When do you believe the sealed portion of the Book of Mormon will be revealed?"

"Oh, that's an easy one," Amelia said immediately. "I'd invite Jesus Christ."

"Of course," Dad agreed. "Anyone would. But who else? Who'd be your second and third choices to get a full dinner conversation going?"

"That's a little harder," Gordon mused. "Maybe one of the Three Nephites."

"But we might get to meet them any old time," said Mom. "I'd invite Ammon or Alma the Younger."

"I'd invite the brother of Jared," said Amelia.

"I'm going to be the wild card," said Carmen. "I'd ask Shakespeare to come." Her secular response gave me a little hope. I looked at her face to try to read it.

"Shakespeare?" asked Mom, laughing. "Whatever for?"

Carmen shrugged. "He could write some good plays about Mormonism," she replied. "I'm sure that would help people in Spirit Prison finally see the light."

Mom nodded thoughtfully. My heart sank a little.

"What about you, Drew?" asked Dad.

I wanted to say I'd invite Moroni and ask if he'd actually been to the temple this week, but instead I said, "Maybe Galileo."

"Galileo!" Amelia burst out laughing. "What could you possibly talk about at dinner? He doesn't even speak English."

"I speak Italian," I reminded her, having served a mission to Rome. "Besides, do you speak Reformed Egyptian?"

"The Nephites didn't speak Reformed Egyptian," she countered. "They just wrote it to save space on the plates. And the brother of Jared wasn't a Nephite anyway."

"And you speak whatever language he did speak?" I pressed.

"I'm sure these guys all have the gift of tongues by this point," she replied. "I still want to talk to someone from the Book of Mormon."

"Why Galileo?" asked Dad.

I savored a bite of sweetened apple before replying. "Do we get just one person to invite in addition to Jesus?" I asked. "I'd like Isaac Newton, too. Maybe Plato. And Darwin. And Michelangelo."

"Michelangelo!" sputtered Amelia. "He was gay!"

"But Darwin's a good choice," said Gordon. "Jesus could set him straight."

"I'd still like to talk to Shakespeare," Carmen repeated. "And perhaps Jane Austen. She could write some good Mormon novels for everyone awaiting the Resurrection. They must have plenty of time to read up there." She paused for a moment. "Must be nice." Carmen had agreed to work until she became pregnant.

The conversation continued several more minutes, Dad looking on with a contented expression on his face. Finally, he said casually, "No one's mentioned Joseph Smith." He licked his fork and set it on his plate. Everyone suddenly looked stricken at the omission.

"Oh, I'd definitely like to meet Joseph Smith," said Amelia quickly. "And Brigham Young, too."

"And Emma Smith," added Carmen. "And Mary Magdalene. And Adam and Eve. And Sarah and Rebecca and King David and...and everybody." Everyone started adding every scriptural name they could think of, every important figure from Church history.

After the talking subsided again, Dad said softly, "You should all come to the temple more often." He paused and looked into the eyes of each of us, one at a time. "The veil is really thin when you're in the temple all the time." He nodded. "Really thin."

I looked about the table, watching everyone stare at my father with respect and admiration. I couldn't believe we were even talking about this. At best, Moroni had been a practical joke. At worst, my father had been set up to witness his miracle. I wanted to speak up and say so. But how could I ruin a pleasant dinner party with my own negativity? Believing these things made my family happy, and happiness was a hard thing to achieve in a world full of despair. It would be hateful of me to try to damage that.

But did that mean I had to be miserable myself by enduring their delusions in silence? I took another sip of milk. Perhaps it did.

Mom refused to let Carmen or Amelia help clear the table. Finally, after another quarter hour, my sister went to retrieve her jacket, and Mom ran to get the rest of the coats from the spare bedroom. "I'm so happy all of you could come tonight," she gushed at the door. "I can't wait till next month!"

Amelia and Gordon hugged Mom and Dad goodbye and then hugged Carmen and me as well. Then Carmen and I hugged Mom and Dad and headed for our car parked at the curb. After making sure Carmen was buckled up, I started the ignition. "I just love your family," she said as we drove past a car still covered with yesterday's snow.

"They're your family, too," I reminded her.

"I'm so glad." She was smiling happily.

I nodded in resignation. This was my lot in life. There were certainly worse ones. I only had to think of the nightly news to realize that. I reached over and squeezed Carmen's hand for a brief moment before returning both hands to the steering wheel. I thought I'd go ahead and tell her we'd have sex tonight without a condom, make her smile even more brightly. But instead, without even meaning to, I started telling her what I really thought about God and Jesus and Moroni. She didn't say anything in return, and I didn't look over to see the expression on her face. I just kept looking straight ahead through the foggy windshield as I drove carefully through the icy, dark streets toward home.

Patty Lou Soils Herself

It was July 25, blisteringly hot in Meridian, Mississippi. Patty Lou looked out the screen door onto the porch. Two calico cats were sleeping lazily in the shade next to the swing. There was a wasp nest on the underside of the swing, so no one could use it until someone knocked the cursed thing off.

Not that there was anyone to use it. Patty Lou hadn't sat on the swing in probably two years, not since Lester had died. Her only daughter, Marsha, and her family lived in Memphis, only coming to visit once every other year on Christmas. Her son, Nathan, lived just five miles away and came by once a month. Tomorrow was her birthday, though, so Nathan was bound to make a special visit, even if his wife didn't stop by with him. His kids were grown and moved out and rarely stopped by, either. Patty Lou spent most of her day reading the newspaper. She'd read half in the afternoon after it came in the mail, and the other half the following morning while waiting for the next day's news. Other than that, she spent most of her time sitting on the sofa and looking out through the screen door. Sometimes, a chicken would walk by. She only had a few left. Raccoons or foxes or wild dogs had gotten the rest.

There was nothing to watch on television, nothing to do. It was hardly worth turning eighty, she thought. Why didn't the Lord simply take her? She was ready to go.

"Endure to the end." It was what the Church always taught. She'd been such a good girl all her life, a good Mormon in the evangelical Bible Belt where she was treated as if she weren't even Christian. Marsha had married a non-member and left the Church as soon as she turned eighteen. Nathan had married another Mormon, but they'd stopped going to church by the time their firstborn was in kindergarten. That left just her and Lester on the path to the Celestial Kingdom, and it was a lonely path. The Church was all about family, but what would it be like to make it to the presence of God without your children or grandchildren in tow?

Patty Lou had always thought if she lived long enough, she'd finally see her kids return to the fold. Now she was turning eighty, and there was no more hope today than when she was fifty. "Please, Heavenly Father, show me a sign," she prayed as she watched one of the cats absentmindedly swat at a fly that kept lighting on its nose. A rooster crowed somewhere behind the old barn.

It was hot and sticky in the house. Patty Lou had never wanted an air conditioner. It made a person weak. The kids said that was why they never visited in the summer. And they never came in the winter because her only heat was the fireplace. The house had been built in the 1940's, a cute little house, even now. There was a spot on the living room floor that looked like termite damage, but Patty Lou couldn't afford to do anything about it. She'd only be around a few more years anyway. And no one wanted the house. What did it matter?

Patty Lou looked at the clock on the mantel. Just past 1:00. The mailman should have passed by now. Maybe there was a birthday card waiting for her. Something other than junk mail and bills. Since Lester died, she hadn't been able to go to church. As a woman, she'd never learned to drive. Her Visiting Teachers came by every few months, but they were young women Patty Lou didn't know, and their visits always seemed more about checking her off a list than really getting to know her.

Still, it was human contact. Her nearest neighbor, Betty Lee, who lived just a third of a mile away, stopped by once a week to bring her to the grocery. Her next nearest neighbor was a mile beyond that. It was nice of Betty Lee to help, but she always tried to get Patty Lou to accept Jesus as her savior. She was being a *missionary* to Patty Lou. It drove Patty Lou crazy.

She pushed open the screen door and stepped out onto the porch. The wood along the front edge was splintered and decaying. Someone was going to trip on that one of these days. The left side of the porch behind the swing was sagging, looking as if it might fall off onto the ground at any moment. There were three more wasp nests along the roof. The wasps had that reddish tint to them that showed they were the bad kind.

Patty Lou walked down the cement steps and crossed the yard. The grass needed mowing. Maybe she'd ask Betty Lee if her son could do it this weekend. Patty Lou had seen a snake in the yard last week. She didn't get close enough to tell if it was a moccasin or just a king snake. She hated any kind of snake. Made her think of the devil in the temple film, a thought which made her wish she could go back to the temple once more before she died. The grass had grown up around the rusting Volkswagen Beetle, Lester's old car, a faded baby blue. The windshield was so dirty now she could hardly see into the car anymore.

She reached the gravel driveway and began walking. It was a good three hundred feet to the paved road where the mailbox was situated. It was surrounded by honeysuckle which always had more wasps flitting around. Patty Lou listened to the birds chirping, the steady hum of insects in the woods to her left and the overgrown field on her right. Up high in the air were three buzzards circling slowly. Patty Lou sniffed the hot air. Whatever had died hadn't died very close by. That was a relief. There was a pack of wild dogs that roamed the area. People had thrown away dogs they no longer wanted and those dogs had united together to survive. Now they were no better than a pack of wolves. There were reports of young calves being killed. One boy nearby had been attacked, but his mother had driven the dogs away with a gun.

At least there had been no bears or panthers spotted in the past few years. That was progress, wasn't it?

Sometimes, Patty Lou missed country life the way it used to be back in the old days. Lazy days fishing in the creek. Blackberry picking in the summer. Now everyone just bought jam at the store. Frozen fish sticks in a box.

Patty Lou was about halfway to the mailbox when a large grayish brown rabbit darted suddenly across the driveway. It so startled her that she stumbled and fell down onto the gravel, tearing her pants and skinning her knee, skinning her left hand, too. There was a pop and immediate searing pain.

She'd broken her hip.

Patty Lou tried to get up, but the pain was excruciating. She just couldn't do it. She was right at the bend in the driveway, so no one could see her from the road. Not that anyone would have been looking anyway. What in the world was she going to do? "Heavenly Father, please help me."

It would be another day and a half before Nathan stopped by for her birthday. Would she have to lie here till then?

What choice did she have?

But fifteen minutes later, lying in the blazing sunshine, Patty Lou knew she'd never last the rest of the afternoon in this unrelenting heat. She was going to have to do something. It was probably a little closer to crawl to the road than to the house, but there was no guarantee anyone would pass by anytime soon.

Better to go back to the house and call for help. She dug into the sandy gravel with her fingers and pulled herself around so that she was facing the house. It felt as if someone were stabbing her. Sweat was already pouring from her face, and she'd just begun.

Patty Lou wasn't a strong woman, though she did still carry her own logs to the fireplace in the winter. She did still carry her own groceries. She did still feed the chickens. But pulling her body along the orange gravel was harder than any of those tasks. She had to cross a trail of ants at one point, and she could feel the stings as she inched along. At least it wasn't an entire bed of fire ants. That would have probably killed her.

"Heavenly Father," she prayed out loud, "is this the end? Have I finally made it?" She hoped to be taken home. She wanted to see Lester again. Maybe God had made her fall as a birthday present to her. All her trials might finally be over.

She stopped crawling and sighed. Perhaps she should just let the inevitable happen. No one could last six hours in this harsh, desert-like sunshine. It must be 95 today. And six hours of misery wasn't as bad as what Lester had had to endure with his bone cancer. She was getting off easy.

Patty Lou wished she could have been a missionary in her younger days, done something exciting with her life, something one could never regret. But girls weren't going on missions back then. She could have gone to France or Norway or Japan. Maybe she should have moved to Salt Lake and married there. Her kids would surely have stayed in the Church then. Had she failed them by trying to stay and build up Zion out here?

Marsha and Nathan wouldn't even miss her. They'd feel all inconvenienced to have to come to her funeral, would be glad that would be the end of their visits. She'd be doing them a favor by dying. Doing them a favor and herself, too.

Patty Lou blinked. The heat was unbearable. She could tell she was already beginning to burn. The ant bites burned and itched. Sweat kept running into her eyes. It stung.

And she really had to go to the bathroom. Why hadn't she gone before she left the house? She shook her head in disgust. It would be mortifying for someone to find her body after she'd soiled herself. She just couldn't have that. Maybe she'd better try to get back to the house after all. If Heavenly Father was kind, he'd still let her die in the hospital. Lots of people died in the hospital these days.

Patty Lou dug her fingers into the gravel again and started pulling herself forward once more. She could hear rustling in the trees and bushes off to the side of the driveway. If it was the dogs, they'd have already come for her, but they still might not be far off. She didn't want to be eaten alive.

She looked up. At least the buzzards would wait till she was dead.

A grueling hour later, Patty Lou had reached the yard. Her clothes were ruined. Just thirty more feet to the front porch, though. She could do it. The grass felt so soft and cool after the blazing gravel. She felt a few more bites from random insects, probably more ants, and then halfway to the porch, she stopped dead still. The grass was moving ahead of her. She hoped whatever it was would go away.

But a moment later, she saw it. A snake, staring right at her. She didn't know what to do. Should she yell and beat the grass to scare it away? Maybe a snake bite wouldn't hurt too much. She'd die a lot quicker than she would from the heat. It could still be a blessing from God. She stared at the snake for a full minute, and the snake stared back. Then it slowly slithered away.

Patty Lou realized she'd wet herself. The warm liquid made her clothes clump annoyingly around her waist. How could she face the world after something like that? "Please, Heavenly Father, take me now." She could feel she needed to relieve herself in another manner, too, one that would force Nathan to put her in a nursing home if he found her. She shook her head. She tried to will herself to die.

"Endure to the end."

She *had* to fight. What would happen if she lived a good life for seventy-nine years, three hundred and sixty-three days, and then gave up on the last day? She'd lose out on the Celestial Kingdom. After all that effort. She *couldn't* give up.

Patty Lou dug her fingers into the grass and inched forward, the sweat and dirt stinging her wounds. There was a big root from the tree in the front yard to pull herself over. She crawled across some fresh chicken droppings, hearing barking in the distance. Multiple barks from multiple dogs. But some of her neighbors had more than one dog. It didn't necessarily mean the wild pack was anywhere around. The sun was still beating down, casting the tree's shadow in the other direction. A few flies flitted about her face, trying to drink her sweat. Even a wasp lit on her to get at the moisture. She stayed still so as not to anger it.

She could smell the urine. In this humidity, the dampness wouldn't dry for an hour or longer, despite the heat. She kept pulling herself forward and finally reached the steps, pausing to catch her breath. The barking wasn't quite so distant anymore. Maybe it was another neighbor's dogs.

"Don't let me be eaten alive," she prayed. "I've been good. Don't be a bastard, Heavenly Father."

Patty Lou bit her lip. How could she talk to God in that manner at a time like this?

The next few minutes were the worst of Patty Lou's life. All the pain of the day was nothing compared to crawling up those three cement steps. Surely, the agony alone would kill her, she thought.

But it didn't. The jagged boards dug into her skin through her clothing, but she was finally on the porch. The cats looked at her and yawned. One of them came up to sniff her face for several moments and then trotted casually off the porch to go somewhere else where she wouldn't be disturbed. The other stared at her for a long moment, scratched behind its ear at a flea, and then licked her paw. A few wasps buzzed around but seemed to ignore her. A persistent fly kept landing on Patty Lou's cheek.

"How much longer, Heavenly Father?" she asked. "Till I'm eighty-five? Ninety? When can I come home?" Her chest was hurting from all the exertion, and for a brief moment, Patty Lou thought she was having a heart attack, like her own mother had had all those years before. This led to a panic attack when she was absolutely sure she was dying, and she suddenly became very dizzy, feeling her head spin in circles. "What if none of it's true?" she thought desperately. "What if I've been wrong all these years?" She clawed frantically toward the edge of the screen door but couldn't quite reach it. "What if the Baptists were right? What if I'm going to Hell?"

Patty Lou had never wanted to live so much in her life. She thrust herself forward with the last of her energy and grabbed the screen door. She yanked it open, and the cat scooted inside immediately before the opportunity was gone. Patty Lou dragged herself into the house, sighing in relief when she heard the door flap shut behind her.

She was safe now. Only ten more feet to the phone.

The smell of the urine was stronger in the house. She wouldn't call Nathan or his wife. She'd call 9-1-1. The paramedics wouldn't tell on her.

Crawling on the floor wasn't as painful as being outside had been, but it was harder to get traction. Still, it was only a few minutes later before she reached the telephone. She dialed. "What is the nature of your emergency?" a monotone voice asked her. Patty Lou explained, and the woman assured her in a bored manner that help was on the way.

She'd made it, she thought. She'd made it. She'd done her duty and not given up. Now it didn't matter if she died.

Only it did matter. Lester's death hadn't made her question things the way the possibility of her own was doing. She wondered if she should ask Betty Lee to take her to the Baptist church just down the road once she was able to walk again. Should she demand her Visiting Teachers drive miles out of their way to bring her to the Mormon church on the far side of town? She'd believed all these years. But believing wasn't the same thing as knowing. What if you believed something that wasn't true? What then happened on the Other Side? Surely, there was no consolation prize for those rooting for the wrong team.

Maybe she was just proving that she'd never been a true Latter-day Saint all those years. So many years. And ready to abandon her faith after one afternoon of tribulation. She shook her head. She was just pooping all over her own soul. She looked about worriedly, wondering that someone had overhead her vulgar thoughts.

Patty Lou's chest was still hurting. Her bites were burning and itching. She was still drenched in sweat, beginning to stink. She looked up toward the ceiling, her eyes narrowing.

What kind of a God treated an old woman like this?

Then she caught her breath. What if there was no God at all, she thought abruptly. A whole new world of possibilities flooded into her mind, none of them good. She put her hand on her chest and rubbed in small circles, waiting, waiting, waiting until she heard the sharp, comforting sound of the siren approaching slowly in the distance.

To Serve God

"Another care package from your Mom," said Sister Alario, looking over my shoulder. "What did you get this time?

"What did *we* get, you mean," I corrected my missionary companion. I held up the first items. "Two Snickers bars. One for me and one for you. Two Reese's peanut butter cups. Two packs of Jello. Two jars of Nutella. And two CDs of The Piano Guys."

Sister Alario laughed. "You Mom sure believes in sharing, doesn't she, Sister Kimball?"

"My Mom would be a saint even if we weren't all saints already just for being LDS."

My family was one of the best in the Church, and I knew it. My mother had served as Relief Society president after my father finished his stint as bishop, and then my father was called to be the stake president. Just a year after that, I was called on a mission to Paraguay at nineteen, and six months later, my brother was called to serve in the Philippines when he turned eighteen. My two younger sisters and younger brother were still at home, the two oldest excelling in Seminary, and the youngest having already read the Book of Mormon twice. Everyone in the family seemed to have a testimony without even trying. I'd read that adversity was the testing ground for faith, but our faith was strong even without it.

We were a special family.

Of course, my Mom had developed diabetes shortly before my call, and I realized even we weren't immune from trials. When I'd expressed my concerns to Elder Swanson, one of the Twelve Apostles visiting our stake in Denver the week I was set apart, he gave me a special blessing. "Your family will be safe while you are on your mission. In fact, they'll be safe *because* you're on your mission. The Lord will protect them in return for your faithful service." The promise of an apostle. The promise of *the Lord*. I had wanted to be a dedicated missionary even before that. Unlike the boys, there was no point for a girl even to go if she wasn't serious about the work. But I promised Heavenly Father to work even harder, to pay him back for paying me back.

I'd taught twenty-one people here in Paraguay that the elders had then baptized. I talked to people on the street, I talked to people on the bus, I talked to people in their homes, bearing my testimony with a smile. I'd gotten along with all of my companions so far, and I had to say, these past fourteen months had been the happiest of my life. And that was saying something when I came from such a happy home. I planned to attend Brigham Young University when I returned to the U.S., study Nutrition, and specialize in developing fantastic meals for diabetics.

The faithful always turned trials into achievements.

"What's the plan for this afternoon?" asked Sister Alario, looking at her watch.

I looked at the jar of Nutella in the box and picked it up. "Why don't we make a special visit to the Giménez family?" I suggested. "They're wavering, but it's Anna's birthday tomorrow, and if we give her a jar of Nutella, she may lead the whole family to the baptismal font. She's the matriarch, after all."

"But that treat's for you," protested my companion. "Your mother wanted you to enjoy it."

I laughed. "They say 'a moment on the lips, a lifetime on the hips.' But think of it this way—'a lifetime on the hips, or an eternity of bliss.' I'd enjoy this treat more if it helped bring a wonderful family into the gospel."

Sister Alario nodded. "But it's okay if I eat mine, isn't it?"

"Of course it is." I laughed again. "And I promise I won't even sneak a spoonful."

"I'll be watching," she said with a smile.

It's funny how you remember what your life was like just before it changed forever. It was like the scripture that says even the wicked are good to their friends. It's how we treat those who aren't our friends that counts. In the same way, it was easy to be good when life had always treated me so well. It was how I'd respond to difficulty that would show my true character.

I wished I could go back to opening that box.

I had bought some pretty cards at a stationery store a few days earlier, and I quickly wrote out a sweet note for Anna to accompany her gift, showing it to my companion for her approval.

Just then, there was a knock on our apartment door. We didn't often get visitors, but sometimes, the zone leaders stopped by for one reason or another. They weren't actually allowed inside the apartment, not so much to help us avoid temptation, but to avoid the appearance of scandal. We'd all stand at the open doorway when they came and talk.

I looked through the peephole. "It's the mission president!" I exclaimed. I looked at Sister Alario, who was frowning.

"An emergency transfer?" she whispered. Sometimes, another companionship in the mission was having personality problems and a special transfer was required to keep the missionaries from killing each other. I hoped that wasn't the case today. I'd been with Sister Alario six weeks and really liked her. I was hoping we'd have another couple of months together.

I opened the door. President Hartman and his wife stood there looking devastated. Had something happened to my brother in the Philippines? "Come in, President," I said. "Come in."

Sister Hartman rushed into the apartment and hugged me, crying. My heart started beating faster. Sister Hartman was squeezing so tightly I could hardly breathe. The president came in and softly shut the door behind him. "What—what is it?" I managed to ask when I could catch my breath.

"We have some bad news," said the president quietly. I nodded for him to continue. He took a deep breath. "Your family...there was a drunk driver." He shook his head. "The drunk driver hit your family's minivan, knocked it over the railing on a steep hillside." He looked at his wife, who was wiping her eyes.

"Well?" I demanded.

"They were all killed," President Hartman said simply. "All of them. Your mother and father and your three siblings."

Sister Alario screeched, but I stood there in silence. "How can this be?" I said, almost to myself.

"Naturally, we'll be flying you home," said the president.

I didn't know what to think. Normally, if a family member died, missionaries were not allowed to go home for the funeral. While we were allowed to email once a week, we were only allowed to call twice a year. Going home for any reason was unheard of. Then it dawned on me.

"My father's not paying for my mission," I said. "I saved all my money myself."

President Hartman shook his head. "I know you're in shock. This is a terrible tragedy. You and your brother will both go back home to Denver. In a few weeks or a few months, if you want to finish your missions, you can come back."

Sister Alario grabbed me and cried into my shoulder. I stared into the mission president's face. He smiled grimly in return.

"Sister Alario," I said, "go visit the Giménez family today as we'd planned. You'll want to call one of the local sisters to go with you."

"Oh, Sister Kimball."

"I'll be packed in ten minutes, President."

On the flight home, I thought about Elder Swanson's promise. Was he a fallen prophet, I wondered? How could he say what he'd said, and then this happen? Maybe my father had committed some terrible sin that negated Swanson's promise. Perhaps my mother had.

That was ridiculous. Besides, the promise should have kept them alive long enough to repent, given my service. Was I not working hard enough to please the Lord? Was this all my fault?

I vowed I wouldn't let hardship turn me away from God. If anyone was to blame, it was me. I'd had things too easy, hadn't built my testimony the way I should have. This was an opportunity for growth, because the Lord loved me.

I looked over across the aisle at an old Catholic woman, clearly afraid of flying, her eyes closed as she rubbed a bead on her rosary.

There were movies to watch aboard the plane, but as I was still technically a missionary, it was forbidden for me to view them. I listened to my CD of The Piano Guys and thought about my mother. She'd given me weekly reports on her exercise and diet. She'd lost twenty-three pounds over the past year. It wasn't a lot, but she believed in taking things slow and steady. She was an example in every way possible. She bore her testimony that she was growing closer to God because of her illness. The diabetes was a blessing.

A thought came into my head of a woman we'd taught a month ago, who said she was grateful when her husband beat her once in a jealous rage because it proved he really loved her.

I shook my head in irritation. It wasn't the same thing. Heavenly Father *did* give us trials for our own good. It was the whole basis of the Plan of Salvation. I'd taught that lesson four times just in the past month. I knew it was true with every fiber of my being.

I looked again at the woman still clinging onto her rosary. Then I closed my eyes and tried to get some sleep.

The current Relief Society president came to pick me up at the airport. I was released from my mission by the first counselor in the stake presidency, and then Sister Grisham drove me home.

"Albert!" I said as my brother opened the door.

"Hi, Sarah." We hugged.

"What are we going to do?" I asked.

"I'm sure Dad left a will. We'll be taken care of."

I shook my head. "I didn't mean that. I meant...I meant...everything."

"The stake's already arranged for the funeral. Apparently, a whole family dying, and two of the kids being off as missionaries has made a big splash in the news. They're expecting a few thousand people to attend."

"What?"

"Of course, most of the stake will be there since Dad was stake president. But lots of non-members will be there, too."

I supposed I was happy that my family was so well-loved and respected, but I kind of wanted to be alone with them right now.

"I think it will be a great missionary opportunity," said Albert. "I'm going to give the main talk at the funeral, and I'm going to incorporate the missionary lesson on the Plan of Salvation."

I looked at him.

"Mom and Dad's deaths could help bring a couple of dozen people into the Church. Maybe more."

I didn't know what to say.

"Elder Swanson has come down for the funeral, too. Can you imagine? Just for us. And he told me he thought I could keep serving my mission for the next few weeks by blogging about all this, using social media to spread the gospel, and then go back to Manila."

"Elder Swanson?" I asked weakly. "But he lied. He told us our family would be safe while we were away." I scratched my arm hard enough to leave a mark. I'd just spoken ill of the Lord's anointed.

Albert took my hand. "Sarah, they *are* safe. They're with Heavenly Father now, where nothing can hurt them." He smiled.

I pulled away. "Well, wouldn't they also be safe with Heavenly Father if someone had shot them all in the head? Why is this any better?"

"We all have our set time here on Earth."

"They were taken *early*!" I insisted. "Or do you think Heavenly Father encouraged that driver to drink?"

"The Lord works in mysterious ways."

"Elder Swanson lied." I drew my fingernails across my arm again.

Why was I being so negative? I needed to repent. This trial was supposed to help me be a better saint. Albert had the right attitude. Elder Swanson had just had an off day. Even apostles couldn't be inspired every single minute of their lives. It didn't mean he was a bad man. I certainly had my occasional moments when I wasn't inspired.

Like right now.

"Elder Swanson said what he had to say to get you to go to Paraguay. The Lord needed you in Paraguay."

I thought about Sister Alario, and Sister Kirk, and Sister McLean, and Sister Lopez. Every one of my companions had been wonderful. My mission had been one of the best experiences of my life. I wanted to go back right now. Why had the Lord taken me away from something I loved? Why had he taken away the family I loved? I didn't understand.

We see through a glass darkly.

I felt I was trying to read the Book of Mormon in the original language. I just didn't understand the words. What could be the meaning behind that odd writing?

"Well, we've got to get ready," Albert said. "The funeral starts in another couple of hours. You'll want to prepare a few words, too."

"Why is everything happening so fast?" I put my hands on my head.

"I've already talked to Elder Swanson. I'll be going right back to my mission within a month. You'll probably want to stay here permanently and take care of the dogs. You only had four months to go anyway."

I looked about, realizing Shelby and Stinger weren't here.

"They're in a kennel right now. The first counselor brought them the other day."

I let out a burst of air in frustration. No one could even bother to pet sit? Sheesh. Then I bit my lip for being ungrateful. I was going to have to come up with something inspirational and uplifting in the next few minutes, show the world that we were still a faithful family, perhaps talk about our being reunited in heaven later. I looked down at my dress. All wrinkled from the long flight, but there was no time to change.

"How long do I get to speak?" I asked.

"Just two or three minutes. My own talk will be a good thirty minutes, and we can only hold people's attention for so long." He smiled. "The media will be there. We'll reach thousands of people beyond those who show up. Mom and Dad would be proud."

"And Karen and Kim and Patrick." Part of me knew my brother was right. I was one of the top missionaries in my mission, not just among the sisters but including all the elders as well. I understood what he was saying. And I was mature enough to grasp the concept of looking at the bigger picture.

I just didn't like being lied to.

It wasn't a lie, I told myself. He misspoke.

I walked to the kitchen and opened the refrigerator. We always used to have orange juice, but it had been too much of a temptation for Mom, so there was none in there now. I grabbed a vanilla Premier shake and twisted off the top. Thirty grams of protein. I needed it. I swigged the liquid down. I carried my suitcase up to my room and opened it, pulling out my notebook. I sat, looking at my Spanish scriptures and my folded missionary outfits, the sacred white garments I wore underneath my dresses, my journal.

I'd had the best fourteen months of my life, and I might not have gone if Elder Swanson hadn't said what he had.

I opened my notebook and began jotting down some ideas for the funeral. A little later, Albert knocked on my door. "Time to go," he said. "Sister Grisham's here to drive us to the stake center." I tore a page out of my notebook and stood up.

The stake center was only ten minutes away, and the parking lot was already full. Hundreds and hundreds of people were there. People hugged us and shook our hands. A few photographers took pictures. Albert led me to the podium, past the five closed caskets, where I sat next to Dad's two counselors. One of them would likely be called as the new stake president in the next few days. Elder Swanson walked in just five minutes after we did, and suddenly all the attention thankfully diverted to him.

Albert leaned over and whispered. "The first counselor is conducting. You'll say a few words, I'll give my talk, and then Elder Swanson will conclude. People all over the Church are going to know about this."

I nodded.

There was a peaceful hymn, a lovely prayer, and then it was my turn to say a few words. I walked up to the podium, feeling the missionary confidence I'd felt in Paraguay starting to return. I looked out over the packed room. Even the back partitions had been opened and chairs set up in the Cultural Hall. More people were here than at stake conference. I'd spoken several times in Asunción and Ciudad del Este, and of course I'd spoken all my life in Sacrament meeting. But my hands were still trembling. I couldn't read the paper.

Was it the Spirit I was feeling?

"Brothers and Sisters," I began, "we're here to remember the lives of my mother and father and brother and sisters. They were all wonderful people." I paused, afraid to go on. Would there be a drunk driver in my own future? I had to act as if every day were my last. I gritted my teeth, looking out at friends and strangers. I *had* learned something from all this. "I remember growing up watching reruns of *The Twilight Zone*. There was one episode where benevolent aliens come to take Earthlings to a better life on another planet. The only thing the humans can translate is the title of a book the aliens always seem to carry. It's called *To Serve Man*. Everything seems great, and the humans do whatever the aliens say. Until the end, when one of the scientists tries to stop another one from boarding the spaceship. '*To Serve Man*,' she cries out, 'It's a cookbook!'"

There was a slight buzz among the audience, people unsure where this little anecdote was going. I could hear Albert tapping his foot somewhere behind me. I'd already spoken longer than he'd wanted. But I had just one more thing to say.

"Brothers and Sisters, when someone tells you they want to serve God, and they hope you'll do your part, I hope you'll think about what I've said."

There was a collective gasp from the crowd, and Albert leaped up, grabbing my arms and pulling me back to my seat. I looked over at Elder Swanson calmly, and he was staring back at me with an expression that suggested he wasn't filled with harmonious love at the moment. But that was the best talk I'd ever given. I was sure of it. The faithful always turned trials into accomplishments. I returned Elder Swanson's glare with a smile.

"My sister's in shock," I heard Albert addressing the audience. "Please forgive her." He stumbled over his next words, and his missionary discussion didn't go as well as he'd hoped. I admit I was grateful for that.

Elder Swanson tried to save the event with his own words at the end, but even he couldn't reclaim the crowd. I didn't really listen very much to what he had to say. I sat in my seat, looking out at those who'd come to see the show. I started thinking about some recipes I could include in the cookbook I still planned to write for my mother, the cookbook she would have enjoyed, had the word of an apostle been something anyone could ever have faith in to begin with.

Best Christian Example

I was the only boy in my high school's Christian Club. I was afraid that being among an otherwise exclusively female group made me look gay, but as the solitary Mormon in a Baptist high school, I had to do everything I could to prove that Mormons were not only Christians but also *good* Christians. Belonging to the Christian Club was one way to do that. Another was by being an A student, even if I wasn't the Valedictorian. Linda, the sole Catholic in our class, was Valedictorian. As an "idol worshipper," she wasn't considered a real Christian either, but she didn't care.

"So at this week's Chapel service," said Mrs. Reynolds, the librarian, who was also head of the Christian Club, "I think we really need to do something special to encourage those who aren't saved to come forward and accept Christ as their Savior. Does anyone have any ideas?"

"I could sing a special song," said Valerie. "I have a version of 'Yesterday' where I use the word 'Calvary' in its place."

"Any other ideas?" asked Mrs. Reynolds.

"We could talk about how accepting Jesus has made our lives better," suggested Kelly.

Mrs. Reynolds put her finger on her chin. "I know," she said after a moment. "We'll call forward anyone who wants to accept Christ as their Savior, just like always, but this time all of you can come forward first. It will encourage the others who are wavering to come forward, too. Kind of like priming a pump."

"That's a terrific idea, Mrs. Reynolds," said Kelly.

Valerie frowned.

Soon it was decided among the eight of us that we would all come forward in the next Chapel service tomorrow afternoon. I was a little worried, thinking that doing so might make it look like I hadn't been a Christian all along, and make it appear I was converting to the Baptist faith. But that's what the club was doing, so I agreed to follow their decision.

After our meeting during lunch period, I went back to class. We only had thirty-three students in the senior class, so we were pretty much with the same kids all day, in English, in Algebra II, in History, in Physics, in P.E., in almost everything. I did take Typing as an elective, while most of the others took Study Period. In Home Room this morning, we'd voted on Senior Superlatives. I'd won Most Courteous flat out, but there was still to be a run-off between me and Jose Lopez for Best Christian Example, Baptist despite his Latin name. Jose wasn't well-liked, always carrying his Bible and preaching to everyone. I'd come in second for Most Popular, losing to Steve Berry, so that gave me an edge over Jose.

I really wanted to be Best Christian Example.

I'd placed third in New Orleans for Algebra I in ninth grade, had placed third in the entire state in English in tenth grade, and second in the state in eleventh grade. I'd really hoped to represent Living Truth Baptist High in English again as a senior, but the school administrator, Mrs. Sanford, who was the preacher's husband, didn't like me. So this year she'd made me compete in Typing. I'd actually come in third in the city for that, but I was irked I couldn't have competed in English. It was clear she was afraid to let Mormons shine. It made her prejudice against us look unfounded. It felt odd competing for acceptance on Mrs. Sanford's terms, but what choice did I have?

Despots of Deseret

I wanted to win Best Christian Example.

This morning, we were told to go home and pray about the runoff and be ready to vote again the following morning.

In History immediately afterward, Rebecca had leaned over and whispered, "What year did World War I end?" We were all answering a sheet of questions, allowed to use both our notes and the textbook. It wasn't a test, just in-class homework.

"The same year as the flu pandemic," I whispered back.

"That didn't help."

"Have you tried the book's index?" I asked.

"Do you want me to vote for you tomorrow or not?" she said, laughing.

"Try the index," I repeated with a smile. She stuck out her tongue and turned to the back of her book.

In Physics class right after lunch, we did actually have a test today. Math was not my favorite subject, despite my success in Algebra I as a ninth grader. What my teacher didn't realize in selecting me to represent the school in the city-wide contest was that I'd already had Algebra I in the eighth grade, back when I was attending public school. In fact, it had been an Honors class. I had done poorly, ending up with a D. But taking the class over again in ninth grade, at a much more leisurely pace, I finally caught on to everything.

Physics was different, though. It seemed inherently more difficult, but even if that weren't the case, our teacher was studying at the Baptist Seminary in Gentilly to become a pastor, and his heart was not in the subject. He would stand at the beginning of each class and say, "Read chapter such and such," and then we'd be on our own while he studied the Bible. I understood the importance of studying on my own to make up for any deficiencies a teacher might have, but my heart wasn't in Physics any more than the teacher's was.

"Okay, class," said Mr. Wilkinson, "before I hand out the tests, I want to offer you a bonus question. One of my colleagues at the Seminary stated that Christ would come back to the Earth at the Last Day, but my professor insisted Christ would only come to the clouds and call the good people up. My professor offered *my* class extra credit if anyone could come up with a scripture that said Christ would actually return to the Earth. Anyone know of anything? It's worth ten points on the exam."

Everyone looked at each other in bewilderment. But I'd just learned a verse in my own Seminary class last week that answered this. I raised my hand.

"Yes, Brad?" asked Mr. Wilkinson.

"Job 19:25 says, 'For I know that my redeemer liveth, and that he shall stand at the latter day upon the earth.'"

I looked at the other students, and most of them were staring back with their mouths open. Mr. Wilkinson opened his Bible and read for a moment. "It *does* say that. I'll be…"

"Jiminy Cricket!" exclaimed Gary, a Seventh-day Adventist who played on the football team and who was praised in Chapel one day because he refused to perform on Saturday.

"Watch it!" said Kelly. "You know where they got the J.C. from!"

Mr. Wilkinson handed out the exams, and I suddenly felt significantly less intelligent than I had a moment earlier while quoting scripture. But I had to admit, the question came at a good time. That was sure to influence a few votes the following morning. I caught Jose's eye as the tests were being passed out, and his look was decidedly unchristian. I muddled my way through the exam, grateful for the bonus points.

"It isn't very Christian to be a know-it-all," said Howard as we were leaving the class. He was a Chinese boy who'd become more withdrawn the past couple of years as he felt his difference more keenly. I wasn't sure what his religion was. We also had Nick, a student who was Greek Orthodox. I didn't know if he was considered Christian or not by the Baptists. He sort of flew under the radar. Despite these attempts at diversity, the vast majority of all the students in the school were not only Protestant but definitively white Baptists. Blacks of any religion were not admitted in order to prevent interracial dating. It seemed ridiculous to me. As an exercise of unity, each year Mrs. Sanford would announce that if we all attended services at the church connected to the school on a set Sunday two weeks before Easter, we'd get a whole week off. Otherwise, we'd only get two days. I never attended, going to my own ward instead. I always got evil looks on the Monday Mrs. Sanford gleefully announced my name as the sole holdout and that we'd only be getting the two days of vacation. But really, even if I hadn't been anxious to be a valiant Mormon, I wouldn't have been interested in extortion. Still, I couldn't help but think now that my actions might have jeopardized my chances of becoming Best Christian Example.

The rest of the day passed uneventfully. I didn't consciously try to court any votes for the runoff the next morning, but I was my normal friendly self. When Carl let the skins steal his basketball in Gym class, I told him it could have happened to anybody. When Amy was late getting out of Typing class, I ran out front and made sure her bus didn't leave without her. My own bus was always the last to leave, so it wasn't as if it were any great sacrifice on my part.

At dinner that night, my Dad asked about my day. I didn't tell him about the bonus points in Physics class, but I did mention the tie for Best Christian Example.

"You know, son," he said, stabbing a scalloped potato with his fork, a meal my mother made once a week, "it isn't necessarily the best idea to fit in with Gentiles. We're supposed to be a peculiar people. They aren't *supposed* to like us."

"But I just want them to acknowledge that we're Christian. They keep saying we're not."

"Who cares what they say? They're ignorant."

"Don't you think it's good missionary work to get them to understand the truth?" I persisted. I'd be eighteen in just five more months and be serving full-time as a missionary for the following two years.

"They'll never really like you, no matter what they say."

"But I came in second for Most Popular."

"You didn't come in first, did you? It's because you're Mormon. And you won't come in first tomorrow. You may as well not get your hopes up. And like I say, it's not a good thing to be hoping for to begin with."

I went to my room after dinner and did my Seminary homework first, and then my schoolwork. Before I went to bed, I read a few chapters from Mark. How could people think we weren't Christian?

The following morning as Mrs. Eberhart took roll in Home Room, I wondered if I should be praying to win the runoff or not. We all stood to pledge allegiance to the U.S. flag, and after that, we pivoted and pledged allegiance to the Christian flag. I'd always felt awkward doing it, as that flag had nothing to do with Mormonism and felt quite alien to me, but it had been clear from the start four years earlier that not doing so would make me an outcast. So was I merely trying to fit in with the heathen? Was it like smoking just to be cool?

I wanted to be Best Christian Example in my senior yearbook. Something everyone would see for years to come.

Mrs. Eberhart passed out the ballots, and after she picked them all up, she tallied the votes at the blackboard. I held my breath as she drew each line, scratching off four vertical lines with a diagonal one and moving to the next bunch. Yesterday there had been a tie for first place, but that tie had only been 10 to 10 because thirteen of the other votes had gone to less popular candidates. But now all thirty-three would be tallied just for us two, and with an odd number, it couldn't end up in a tie again.

After a few moments, it was 16 to 16, and the final vote was about to be counted. Please, Heavenly Father, let people see I'm a Christian.

"Jose Lopez is the Best Christian Example for the senior class!" Mrs. Eberhart announced, drawing the final line on the blackboard.

Everyone clapped, and a few people cheered. Rebecca leaned over and whispered, "The rest of us still think you're way cooler than Jose." I forced a smile back at her.

But there was that word again—cool. Was I just drinking a beer behind the garage with the neighborhood kids to fit in?

Classes were five minutes shorter today so that we could squeeze in Chapel after lunch. And it was just as well we had the shorter periods because my attention span was suffering greatly. All I could think about was the vote. Had it been rigged? I did get more votes today than yesterday, but I still couldn't help wondering. And did people really like Jose better, or did they simply not want to vote for a Mormon? Was it bias or just popularity? It *felt* like discrimination, but who could tell for sure?

In the cafeteria, I ate with my friends, and they joked and laughed and told stories as usual, and I began to feel better.

But then Mr. Wilkinson came over to our table. "Hi, Brad," he said with a smile. "I just wanted to tell you I showed that scripture to my professor, and he said it meant that Christ's power and influence will be on the Earth at the last day, not that Jesus himself will be." He paused. "So you don't get the bonus points for your exam. Nice try, though." He clapped me on the back and walked off.

"What an a-hole," said Dennis. "Sheesh."

"Watch it!" said Kelly. "You know where that word comes from!"

I looked at her and thought, *I can't do this anymore.* "Where?" I asked, sipping my root beer. "Jesus? Or shit?"

Everyone at the table stopped talking and stared at me. Finally, Kelly swallowed and said, "That's not the way for a Christian to talk."

I nodded. "But I'm not a Christian," I said. "I'm a Mormon." Though, truth be told, my bishop wouldn't want me swearing, either.

"But...but...I thought..."

"I believe in a living prophet and scriptures written by American Indians."

There was silence for another moment. Then Kelly took a sip of her Coke, and Dennis took another bite of his sandwich.

"Really?" asked Gary. "That's kind of cool. Maybe you should tell us more about that."

I smiled. "I will. But excuse me just a second first." I stood up and walked over two tables to where Mrs. Reynolds was eating with some of the other faculty. I told her I'd resigned from the Christian Club and then I went back to my table. Calmly eating my potato chips, I told my friends about Joseph Smith's First Vision.

Christmas Brownies

It was Christmas and time for my annual visit back to my parents' home in St. George. I'd been close to my folks growing up, and close to my sister Beverly and my brother Jonathan. They were both married now and would be coming with their families as well. It would be a madhouse. I hoped there would be an opportunity to tell my parents what I'd needed to say to them for quite some time. I had to finally come out of the closet. Tell them the truth.

I smoked pot.

I hadn't thought my doing so would change anything, but it had. Now there was this great secret between us, a wall that kept us from fully communicating. While I knew the revelation would hurt them, *not* telling them was hurting them, too. We were growing apart. I had to clear the air and be honest. It was the only way to salvage our relationship.

I drove up to the house, a late Craftsman from about 1920. Mom and Dad had bought the place in the early 1980's, shortly after they married in the St. George temple. Then Beverly had come along, followed by Jonathan and eventually by me a few years after that. I grabbed the three gifts from the back seat of the car, two for Beverly's daughters, Tammy and Ruth, and one for Jonathan's son, Jacob. The adults hadn't exchanged gifts in years.

"Cooper!" said Mom, opening the door, her arms spread wide. She pulled me close and kissed me. I tensed, but apparently the mouthwash successfully covered my usual coffee breath.

"It's so good to see you, Mom."

"Colorado's not that far away, you know. You could visit more often."

"You're welcome to come see me any time you want," I returned.

"And leave Zion?"

"Zion is in Durango, too," I pointed out.

She didn't respond. I went inside and placed the gifts under the tree. The kids immediately picked them up again, struggling to read the nametags before setting them back alongside the other packages. Dad came over to hug me, followed by Beverly. Jonathan gave me a hearty handshake, as did Beverly's husband, Aaron. Robin, Jonathan's wife, just smiled and waved from a distance. I headed back for the front door.

"You're leaving already?" Mom asked jokingly, but with a slight tone of real worry.

"You don't think I'd come without my famous brownies, do you?" I replied.

"You didn't have to do that!"

"This is love in the form of food," I said. "Your chocolate chip cookies, Beverly's raisin oatmeal cookies, and Dad's ham. This is what makes Christmas so special."

"And family," said Mom.

"Especially family," I agreed, laughing. Running back out to the car, I wondered if I was going to be strong enough to do it. It was like pulling a Band-Aid off of my hairy arm. Or stepping into a cold swimming pool. These things needed to be done quickly to get them over with. But I always dragged the experience out, making it worse for me and anyone who had to listen to me moan about it. I picked up the plastic-wrapped plate of brownies and walked back to the house.

It was almost noon, so it wasn't long before the dinner was spread on the table. Ham, sweet potato casserole, green bean casserole with cream of mushroom soup and fried onions, corn, homemade bread, real butter, and two pitchers of strawberry Kool-Aid. Jonathan talked about his work in Salt Lake as an insurance salesman. Enough to make me wish I could run out to the car and eat one of my emergency brownies now. But then Aaron talked about his work in Las Vegas as a police officer. "We pulled over this one guy who was weaving from lane to lane. When he rolled down his window and all the fumes came out, I was afraid *I* was going to fail the drug test."

"That actually happened to him once," Beverly interjected. Everyone laughed.

"How awful," said Mom. "It's hard to get away from the influence of evil." She looked at Robin, who had refused to convert to Mormonism before marrying my brother.

Robin clearly understood the intent of the comment and grabbed another piece of homemade bread, stabbing the butter in the dish a little more forcefully than she needed to. To my knowledge, her biggest sin was coffee.

Why did I still think of perfectly normal, innocent activities as sin? I hated that about the Church. This might be a good time to finally say something, I thought. But just as I was about to open my mouth, Mom spoke up again.

"If only people understood that the Lord was trying to *help* them by telling them what not to do," said Mom. "It isn't to make life difficult for them. It's to make it better."

There was a firm round of consent about the table. Perhaps I shouldn't say anything, after all, I thought. But then, that was the whole problem. Here was a normal dinner conversation, and I couldn't take part in it because I had this big secret. Things were going unsaid that needed to be said. My parents and siblings no longer knew me. And if I let that go on, the increasing distance between us would be my fault.

But if I did say something, there would be a different kind of distance, and perhaps more of it.

I took another spoonful of corn.

The conversation continued. Robin and Beverly talked about things the kids had done. Robin was never one of my mother's favorites, given her non-member status. Mom had told me dozens of times over the phone that she was praying and fasting that one day Robin would see the light and join the Church so that Jacob would be sealed to the family after everyone went to the temple. Mom tried to be nice, not wanting to push Robin away, and yet she managed to do it regularly anyway.

For instance, after we retired to the living room after the meal, Mom grabbed her camera. "Time for a family photo!" she said. She lined Dad, Jonathan, Beverly, Aaron, me, Tammy, and Ruth in front of the Christmas tree. Jacob was deliberately left out, and Mom handed the camera to Robin. The photo was clearly to be only of the family members that counted. The ones who made up the eternal family.

"I'm sure I can set that on a timer so we can all get in the picture," I said.

Mom frowned but didn't have the nerve to be any more blatant than she'd already been. But would she start excluding me from photos, too, if I came out to her? Would she stop asking me to come visit? I didn't want to feel as alienated as Robin must surely feel, and yet I actually felt that way already. Perhaps it was too late to do anything to salvage the relationship in any event. Maybe that's just what happened when kids grew up.

After a series of photos and another half hour of conversation, Mom brought out the plates full of brownies and cookies. Even though we'd all just had a huge meal, we still each stuffed a few more treats down our throats. I stood up and started for the kitchen. "Anyone want..." I stopped when I realized I was about to offer coffee to everyone, and from my Mom's kitchen at that.

"What did you need, dear?" asked Mom with a puzzled look.

"He wants coffee," said Aaron. Mom squealed at the word. "I'm a trained police officer. I know how to smell contraband on someone's breath."

"Contraband!" I laughed.

"Laugh all you want," said Aaron, "but you're no longer worthy to go to the temple, are you?"

"Is it true, Cooper?" asked Mom, with her hand to her mouth. I wanted to brush off a crumb from her cheek.

I nodded. This might be a good way to break the ice. Maybe my brother-in-law had done me a favor. "I've been drinking coffee for more than a year," I said.

Mom looked as if she might cry. I wanted to roll my eyes but had to remind myself that this was serious to her. "Even Joseph Smith drank alcohol," I pointed out.

Mom gasped. "Don't say such things in front of the children." The kids were looking simultaneously bored and sleepy, and anxious to finally get to the presents.

"I drink a pot of coffee a day," I went on. "And I still pay my taxes and I still mow my lawn."

"But do you still go to church?" asked Dad. Mom looked at him in horror for saying it, but then looked back at me in supplication, her eyes begging me to deny the accusation.

The truth was that I'd decided over a year ago to take a break from church. I thought that after a while, I'd start to miss it and would return with a greater appreciation. Instead, I just wanted to get farther away. I liked being able to drink a glass of wine with dinner. I liked sleeping with my girlfriend without shame. Well, I liked that there was a little less shame every day. I might still go back eventually, I told myself, but not for a while yet. "I miss services once in a while," I said, afraid to tell the truth. I felt like a child lying about the cookie jar.

So who said there was no more shame?

"How often is once in a while?" asked Mom.

I smiled. "Every Sunday," I finally admitted.

Now she did start crying. "We're going to miss you in heaven," she said, sniffling. She picked up a napkin from the coffee table and dabbed at her nose. Then in mid-sniff, she suddenly sat up straight and stared at me with her mouth open. "Do you have sex?" she asked. "Do you drink?" She looked about wildly. "Do you—do you—"

"Kill people?" I finished for her with a smile. Her eyes widened, and I continued. "I smoke pot," I said, deflecting the question about sex. Even I knew I could never address that topic.

Mom's eyes flew to the plate on the coffee table. "Did you—?"

"Of course not, Mom. Good grief." I laughed, but I wasn't feeling very mirthful.

"Oh, this is the worst Christmas of my entire life," said Mom, crying again.

I looked at Beverly and Aaron, who were looking at me in disgust. Jonathan was eating a brownie and staring at the tree. Robin was smiling broadly.

"Why don't we open presents?" I suggested.

"The only present I want is for you to repent."

"Tammy," I said, addressing the oldest girl, "go get each kid a present." She leaped up from her spot on the floor and ran to the tree, apparently happy for something important to finally take place today. The next several minutes were taken up by paper tearing and box opening. The kids seemed to like their toys, or at least had been trained to say they did. Training counted for a lot.

That's why I suddenly knew that if I ever did have children, I wouldn't raise them in the Church. There was no way you could let them have two decades of continual influence and then let them "decide" when they became adults. Influence made the decision for them. I was lucky to escape.

If I really had escaped. Why did I still feel the need to justify myself? I *was* a decent person, but every second I spent in my parents' home today had me feeling like an apostate.

I guess I was in fact an apostate. But a decent one. It took distance to realize that distance sometimes was good.

The rest of the afternoon dragged by painfully. While I felt a tremendous relief finally to no longer have secrets, I was unhappy that my freedom came at the cost of my mother's happiness. If one of us had to suffer, shouldn't it be me, after all my mother had done for me?

And yet, I couldn't regret having finally said something. It was *good* to be honest.

"Mom, I'm the same person I always was," I said as I got ready to head back for the hotel. I'd leave for Durango first thing tomorrow morning.

"I know," she said sadly. "That's what hurts the most. All this time I thought you were good. When really…"

How could you love your mother and still want never to visit again? I had lots of good memories of my years in the Church, but I never wanted to visit there again either. Having different goals and ideas wasn't a predetermined part of growing up. Beverly and Aaron still fit in completely both at home and at church. So what was wrong with me? I wondered if maybe I *should* repent.

Under the influence suddenly took on a new meaning.

Mom gave me a hug as I stood at the front door, though it wasn't as close and warm as the one she'd given me earlier. Dad shook my hand. Beverly nodded. Robin squeezed my arm. Just as I was unlocking my car door, Jonathan came out to say something. "Do you have any pot in the car now?" he asked in an officious tone.

"You're not Aaron on patrol," I said. "Let it drop."

"Do you?" he repeated.

I had a baggie full of pot brownies that I'd brought along, just in case I needed something tonight after the revelation. I hadn't wanted to leave them in the hotel in case a maid found them. They were sitting on my front passenger seat. But none of that was any of Jonathan's business.

Still, the whole point of coming out at Christmas was so that I didn't have to lie and hide any longer. "I have four pot brownies," I said sardonically. "Want one?"

Jonathan's brows furrowed and he looked more intense than I'd ever seen him. Was he going to hit me? Call Aaron and make a citizen's arrest? This stuff wasn't legal in Utah like back home.

"Can you spare two?" he asked. When I looked at him in astonishment, he added quickly, "You get to leave, but I'm here for supper, too." He motioned toward the open car door with his chin.

"One for you and one for Robin?" I asked, starting to smile.

"Oh, no, Robin would kill me if she knew. She may be an Episcopalian, but she's a better Mormon than I am. These are both for me. Both right now." He held out his hand. I reached into the car and gave him the whole baggie. He slipped it into his coat pocket.

I felt I understood my brother for the first time. "I love you, Jonathan."

"Thanks, Cooper." I wasn't sure if he was thanking me for what I'd said or what I'd given him.

"I saw the look on Robin's face," I continued. "You should feel free to share." It was bad enough for parents and children to have secrets from each other, but surely it would be intolerable for a married couple. Jonathan patted his coat pocket and frowned, looking over his shoulder toward the living room window. Turning back to me, he looked me in the eyes a long moment and then nodded briefly. He gave me a hug and headed back to the house. I watched the door close behind him. The Christmas lights were still twinkling around the doorway, promising warmth in the fading sunlight. A cardboard snowman was guarding a box full of brightly colored fake gifts off to the right. I heard Christmas music start playing inside the house.

I wondered if I'd ever be coming back. I looked back at the twinkling lights.

For Jonathan and Robin's sake, I would.

I climbed into the car and drove off, hoping to find an open diner where I could have a cup of decaf before heading back to the hotel for the night.

Poison Ivy Testimonies

I had just turned twelve and was finally eligible to participate in Girls Camp. Our stake in Asheville had arranged for us all to spend a week in the Pisgah National Forest. My parents were a little worried because a woman had been raped there a couple of months ago, and a gang of teenagers had tied an old couple to a tree a month before that. But our youth leaders guaranteed that the Holy Ghost would be with us and watch over us, so my parents reluctantly agreed I could take part.

"Hannah," I said into my cell phone, "I'm going!" Hannah had been my best friend since we were Sunbeams.

"That's great, Diana!" she replied. "Julie and Connie will be there, too!" We were all Beehives in our ward. Julie and Connie were a little on the dim side, but nice enough. My mother always chided me if I said anything like that about them at dinner, and I guessed I was in fact a little snooty at times, a weakness I tried steadily to overcome. My teachers at church often tried to single me out by giving me extra opportunities to grow. Julie and Connie sometimes snickered about it. But Hannah, Hannah I liked completely. She was sweet, with dimples, the friendliest smile, wavy auburn hair, and she always had a kind word for others. Her testimony never wavered, while mine did. She was the type to grow up to be Relief Society president one day. I was the type to become someone's service project.

"We're going to get to hike and swim and tell stories around the campfire," I continued.

"But we'll have to sleep in tents," Hannah countered. "They won't spring for the cabins. And we probably won't get to shower for a week."

"No parents, though," I pointed out. "That has to count for something."

"But my sister Victoria will be there," said Hannah. "And she'll report anything I do back to my Mom."

"Well, *I* haven't got a sister," I said. I had a younger brother who was ten and who would be glad to see me go. I couldn't say I would miss Calvin much, either. "And you know I'll keep you out of trouble."

"You always see the positive." Hannah laughed. "What would I do without you?"

Normally during the summer, Hannah and I rode our bikes through the neighborhood, sneaked to the store to buy lipstick which we wiped off before our parents could see, and talked about what life would be like four long years from now when we would finally be allowed to date. I didn't particularly like boys, though, and didn't really mind not going out with them the way the other girls at school did, the way the other girls at church kept wishing they could. Just spending time with Hannah was enough. We slept at each other's house, stayed up late watching 1930's horror movies on DVD, and talked about what we'd do when we grew up. Hannah wanted to marry a returned missionary and have five kids. I wanted to go on a mission myself, maybe to Africa, and become an epidemiologist.

"Too bad you're not a boy," Hannah said once. "You'd make the perfect husband."

I took it as a compliment.

I wondered if anyone would be bitten by a bug out in the woods during Girls Camp and catch a new disease. Part of me thought about how my parents would be upset by such a thing, and part of me was fascinated by the possibility.

The big day was only a week away, and on a bright Monday morning, all the girls met at the stake center. We squeezed into six minivans driven by Young Women's leaders, and we headed for camp about an hour away. The first thing we did was set up our tents, which took quite a while, as not even the adults seemed to know what to do. Brother Campbell, the first counselor in the stake presidency, was setting up his tent by himself. He was the lone male present, here to ensure our safety, in case the Holy Ghost alone wasn't enough. I finished our tent first and then went with Hannah over to help some others, where I heard Sister Bradford talking to Sister Goodson. "I better get a shiny gold doorknob on my mansion in heaven."

Sister Goodson replied with a smile, "I'm happy with just brass."

"Sounds like a Telestial attitude to me," Sister Bradford returned.

"Lusting after gold isn't a Celestial one," Sister Goodson said, smiling back.

This was going to be a great week, I thought, nudging Hannah to listen to the conversation. My parents had talked to me about the perverse satisfaction I had in discovering that people at church weren't perfect. "The Church isn't for the spiritually healthy," my Dad said. "It's for the spiritually ill."

"Then I should be right at home," I replied. "What are you complaining for?"

My parents just looked at each other, not knowing what to say. I felt sorry for them, having such a difficult daughter.

Of course, Calvin was no prize, either.

Being at camp with Hannah was fun. It was a time to forget about parents and the upcoming school year and Gentile friends and television and cell phones. But the realities of the place soon began to take their toll. It was hot. There was no air conditioning. There were bugs. Everyone was covered in mosquito bites by the morning of the second day. I wondered if I had caught some new disease myself. Six of the girls had poison ivy rashes by the end of the third day. The food was terrible, and there wasn't enough of it after hours and hours of hiking every day. We did spend an hour every afternoon playing a Mormon trivia game or singing hymns or doing some role-playing exercises about how to tell our non-member friends about the Church. The worst part, though, was that at night around the campfire, instead of telling ghost stories or doing other fun things, we had to listen to stories about the pioneers crossing the plains. We were in North Carolina, for goodness' sake. What did we need to hear about that stuff for?

Hannah, Julie, Connie, and I made up for it by sharing a tent and staying up past lights out and telling our own stories. "Did you hear the one about the couple that drove to a secluded spot to neck?" asked Hannah.

"Mormons don't neck," said Julie.

"Well, these weren't Mormons. Or at least, the boy wasn't. The girl was, and she said she didn't want to go to any secluded spot. She said she'd heard there was a crazy serial killer out there with a hook for a hand."

"Ooh." Did I mention that Julie was dim-witted?

"But the boy took her out there anyway and tried to start kissing her. She kept pushing him away and he kept trying to fondle her."

"That's just like a non-Mormon boy," said Connie, nodding. She was only six months older than I was and couldn't even go to youth dances yet. And with all our parents monitoring what television shows and movies we could go see, I wondered why she thought she knew anything about this. I at least read books. A library card was a useful thing.

"When the boy kept trying to feel her up," Hannah continued, "she started bearing her testimony. The boy finally got so mad he threw the car into gear and took off back for the girl's house to drop her off. And when she got out of the car, what do you think she saw?"

"What?" breathed Julie.

"A *hook* hanging from the door handle!"

"Ooh!"

"Well, I heard Sister McCullers telling Sister Bradford there might be some bad men roaming the woods at night," I said, not only because it was true but also because I was feeling perverse again and wanted to instigate a little adrenalin flow. "That we ought to be real careful if we have to get up to go to the latrine after dark."

"Do you really think there will be any trouble, Diana?" asked Hannah. "My Mom only let me come because the bishop promised her we'd be okay."

"The Church would never do anything that put us in real danger," I replied, trying not to sound regretful. Perhaps a mission to Africa, though, might pose *some* adventure. And we had all heard about those missionaries kidnapped by evil men in Russia. "Besides, Sister Bradford brought a gun."

"A gun! How do you know?"

"She showed it to me. She told me not to tell anyone. But you guys aren't 'anyone.'"

We talked for another twenty or thirty minutes, but as it had been a long day, we eventually nodded off one after the other. I dreamed about finding a cure for Ebola and then waking up worried I might have diarrhea out here in the middle of nowhere. Or that some of the girls would have their periods and spread disease among the entire group. I was nothing if not morbid. Looking up at the stars at night, I began to wonder whether with such disease all over the world if there was even a God out there to begin with. Perverse. But hopefully, involving myself fully in these church activities would salvage my soul. We held Seminary scripture chases during lunch. I knew almost all of the answers. But knowing the answers didn't mean I didn't still have questions. I tried to throw myself into the physicality of the entire experience, hoping that would help, too. By the end of the fifth day, even hiking and swimming began to grow tedious. I could see that even the adults were ready for the week to be over. I lazily scratched at my own mosquito bites as we started to eat. Not being an idiot, of course, I didn't have any poison ivy to worry about. I tried to psyche myself up for another painful evening of Church history. Halfway through dinner, though, everything changed.

Brother Campbell came running into the camp. We hadn't even noticed he was gone. "Everyone, get up!" he shouted.

"What is it?" demanded Sister Bradford.

"There's an anti-Mormon mob heading this way! They're going to rape all the girls and kill us all because we're Mormon!"

The girls all jumped up, their food spilling everywhere. Hannah grabbed my hand.

"I'll go try to head them off!" shouted Brother Campbell, heading back the way he'd come.

"Come on!" Sister Bradford said authoritatively. "We're going to run up the trail and hide."

"But it's dark out there," whined one of the girls.

"Everyone get their flashlights," Sister Bradford ordered. She went to her own tent and came back with her gun. Hannah squeezed my hand harder.

Within five minutes, we'd abandoned camp. One of the leaders tried to call 9-1-1 but couldn't get a signal. We took off up the trail, huffing because of the incline. After about twenty minutes, we came to a small clearing. The sisters gathered us all around them, made us call out our names, and then ordered us to turn off the flashlights.

There was only a tiny sliver of moon, and everything went black.

"I'm scared," said Julie.

"Diana, what are we going to do?" asked Hannah.

"The Lord will take care of us," I said. I didn't know what was going to happen out here, but I knew I wanted Hannah not to feel afraid.

"Do you really think so?" asked Connie. "I mean, even Mormons die sometimes."

Julie started crying.

I knew I didn't want to die for a religion I wasn't even sure I believed.

"Everyone, hush!" whispered Sister Bradford loudly. "Don't make a peep! If that mob is looking for us, we don't want to give ourselves away. Stay absolutely quiet until I give the word."

We all held hands, standing, afraid to sit. The fear was contagious and kept us from growing tired, even after another twenty minutes had passed. Then we heard it—steps coming along the trail. Lots of steps.

"Shhh!" whispered Sister Bradford. But I could still hear one of the girls sniffling.

After a while, the sound of footsteps dissipated, and another fifteen minutes after that, Sister Bradford turned on her flashlight. "You, Diana," she said.

"Yes?"

"You and I are going back to the camp to see if it's safe to return." She held the flashlight in one hand and her gun in the other. "The rest of you stay here in the dark. And keep quiet."

Hannah grabbed for me. "Don't go, Diana!"

I kissed her on the mouth and then walked over to join Sister Bradford. I felt sorry for my parents. The news was going to be so hard on them. I felt sorry for Hannah, too. She was never going to have another friend who loved her like I did.

And I felt mad at the bishop and the stake president. Weren't they supposed to be inspired?

Sister Bradford and I walked carefully back down the trail to the camp and looked about. Even the one flashlight didn't provide much illumination, and she wouldn't let me turn mine on, afraid the extra light would give us away. We stopped and paused several times along the way and then kept going. The camp was deserted and showed no signs of anyone having been there besides us. After looking into each tent and determining that everything looked okay, we walked quickly back up the trail. This time, I was allowed to turn on my beam.

When we reached the group, Hannah grabbed me and buried her face in my neck. Several of the other girls were crying audibly in relief. Sister Bradford ordered everyone to turn on their flashlights. Turning her own upward to light her face from below, she started talking. "Okay, girls, you can all relax now. There is no anti-Mormon mob. We just wanted you to feel what it means to be Mormon in a world that hates us. We are always under attack in one way or another, and the threat of real anti-Mormon mobs is just one new state or federal law away."

The girls stopped crying and stared at her. Hannah was still holding onto my hand tightly. As I listened to the unbelievable words, I realized I was squeezing hers tightly as well.

"We are always being threatened because of our beliefs," Sister Bradford went on, "and the only way we can be prepared for whatever might happen is by having strong testimonies." She paused and smiled, but because of the way the lighting from below struck her face, it made her grin look macabre. "So let's spend the next hour or so bearing our testimonies here in this clearing before we head back to camp."

"I'll start," said Sister Goodson. She then began bearing her testimony of the truthfulness of the gospel. As I looked about me, I realized that testimonies were contagious, too. And these women knew that.

"I—I don't understand," Hannah whispered to me.

"They were lying," I replied. They must have had some of the priesthood come out to scare us with the footsteps.

"But that's—that's mean," she said.

"Let's make our way to the edge of the crowd," I whispered. "Then we'll sneak away and head back to the camp. Give them a little scare of their own when they realize we're missing."

"What'll we do back at camp all alone?" she asked.

"We'll eat the rest of our dinner and go to bed. I'm exhausted."

We made our way back down the trail. There were enough embers in the pit to get the fire going again, and we finished our interrupted meal. I could see streaks on Hannah's face where her tears had cleared a little of the dust and dirt of the last few days away. Looking at her, I suddenly felt very sad. I wouldn't be seeing her much anymore, as I would no longer be going to church, while I knew she would. I felt sorry for my parents, too, who would never understand why I couldn't go back.

Hannah and I cleaned up our dinner things and then crawled into our tent. I held Hannah's hand as she quickly fell asleep, and I kept holding onto it tightly even after I heard the heavy sound of footsteps coming back loudly down the trail.

A Stupor of Thought

It was 5:00 a.m. on a Monday morning, time to get up and prepare for work. An entire week of drudgery ahead of me. I dragged myself out of bed and made my way to the bathroom in the dark. I hadn't had to get up once during the night to pee. In fact, I hadn't even had to move to the sofa in the middle of the night because I was no longer able to breathe in bed. So it had been a remarkably good evening.

So why was I so unhappy to be waking up?

I began brushing my teeth with PreviDent, the special prescription toothpaste the dentist had sold to me for $12. It was supposed to stop the extreme sensitivity I had with several of my teeth. Over the counter toothpastes designed for this didn't seem to do the trick. I'd only been using this one for a few weeks, and while there was some improvement, my teeth still hurt if I ate anything cold. No cavities in over thirty years, though. My hygienist always said, "You've been a good boy, Tim," as if I were eight years old.

Mickey's teeth looked so white against his dark skin. He had such a beautiful smile. But then, he used a whitener, which I was afraid to use.

I yawned widely into the mirror.

Daylight Savings Time started yesterday, so my body still thought it was 4:00 a.m. That must be the trouble. Of course, I'd napped a lot yesterday and gone to bed at 9:00, so I didn't understand why I was still dragging this morning. The prospect of being with my coworkers all day hung over me like a pall. I spit out the toothpaste but didn't rinse, as per instructions, and then I flossed my teeth. I only flossed once a day, but I made myself do it first thing in the morning to make sure it was done at all. Commandments had to be obeyed, even if they were secular ones, and even if obeyed perfunctorily.

Mickey always obeyed the commandments, even now, after all these years. I still couldn't fathom how the Church used to say Blacks had been "less valiant" in the Pre-Existence.

Well, he did drink coffee, didn't he?

I shook my head. Coffee wasn't a sin, I reminded myself, though the Church still insisted it was. And Blacks were fully equal to anyone else in every way possible, which even the Church now admitted was true. Of course, it was less true here in Pocatello. In church or out.

Now that I'd flossed, it was time for my next biggest chore—weighing myself. I pulled off my white T-shirt and black sweat pants and stood on the scale. 186.5. I shrugged. It meant I'd gained two-tenths of a pound over the weekend, but I could live with that. Of course, the problem with "living with that" was that if I didn't freak and do something about the added weight immediately, I'd have to live with another two-tenths tomorrow. Yes, I'd have to eat lightly today. And take a walk during lunch.

Mickey always kept himself in great shape, spending an hour at the gym every day. He also volunteered with Big Brothers. And mowed our elderly neighbor's yard. And wrote letters to the editor about universal healthcare.

I put my T-shirt and sweat pants back on and headed for my office. It was still pitch black, but I didn't turn on any lights, not wanting to wake Mickey up. He was usually still asleep when I left at 6:00 for downtown. I closed my office door before flipping on the light switch, and then I checked my emails.

Another fifteen in spam overnight, and another twenty-three political emails in my regular inbox. I deleted them all.

I couldn't eat or drink for thirty minutes after brushing my teeth, to give the formula time to work on the nerve endings. Normally, I spent this time fixing myself a sandwich to bring to work for lunch, but I just wasn't in the mood today. Instead, I emptied the coffee grounds from Mickey's coffeepot and refilled the filter with fresh grounds, adding enough water in the back of the coffeemaker to give Mickey six cups this morning. I didn't even like the smell of coffee. But while I had no lingering belief in either Joseph Smith or the Word of Wisdom, I could probably still pass a temple recommend interview. Except for the man on man sex, that is. Then again, it wasn't as if Mickey and I weren't legally married. And even the Church grudgingly accepted interracial marriages these days. Just not gay ones. I slid the glass pot back on its stand. I usually turned the machine on right as I left for the bus. The coffee stayed warm for two hours and would still be ready when Mickey finally woke up.

I sure didn't want to go to work today. I sat on the sofa and pulled a blanket over myself in the dark. I'd relax here for a few minutes before eating a banana for breakfast. I left my office door open a crack to allow a little light into the living room, so I could see my watch and get moving when I had to.

Of course, I could always call in sick today.

We were penalized at work if we called in sick on either a Monday or a Friday, so that wouldn't be a good idea. Plus, with Daylight Savings Time having just started, my manager would be sure to expect the truth, that I was just sleepy. Another option would be simply to sleep a little longer and go in an hour late. We had reasonably flexible schedules. As long as I got my eight hours in, there wouldn't be any trouble.

But wouldn't it be great not to go in at all? In Genesis, God said that a life of toil would for Adam's "sake." Most people thought that meant "as a punishment," but didn't "for your sake" actually mean "for your benefit"?

It must have been a translation error. Work was a curse. I wouldn't wish it on my worst enemy. I didn't want to go downtown today.

Stop it, Tim, I told myself. I was perfectly aware that once I got an idea in my head, I usually ran with it, and I couldn't afford to run with this one. Besides, Mickey's birthday was next Monday, and I was already scheduled to take that day off. I certainly didn't need two Mondays off in a row.

Okay, I'd go in as usual, but I would still rest on the sofa for a bit first. If I missed my regular 6:05 bus, I could take the 6:20. Not the end of the world. I sat up with the blanket over me and closed my eyes. It felt so good.

Our little space heater clicked on and started purring. We didn't have any significant heating system in the house, just one space heater in the living room and one in the bedroom. They drove the electric bill sky high in the winter, and paying the bills was always a problem. I paid the mortgage every month by myself, and I paid the electric bill, the water bill, the gas bill, the internet/phone/cable bill, and 90% of the grocery bill. Plus, I paid for Mickey's health insurance. I'd just paid over $500 in bills the past couple of weeks, and a new water bill had come in the mail Saturday. When I asked Mickey for some help, he said, "That doesn't need to be paid for a couple of weeks yet."

I replied, "And you don't think there will be new bills to pay in a couple of weeks?"

He just said, "Well, I don't have any money to give you right now."

And I'd let it slide. What could I do? Mickey was a self-employed carpenter, and he only had occasional small jobs. At least he was no longer hiding the bills from me as he used to do, and last month, he'd actually given me $250 toward the bills. But that was nowhere near his half of the shared expenses. So I certainly couldn't afford to risk my job by staying home today. I wished my husband would get a full-time regular job, but he simply didn't want to.

Just like I didn't want to go to work today.

If Mickey could be lazy, so could I.

Lazy! I hated myself for even thinking the word.

But if he could do what he wanted, why couldn't I?

Maybe I should pray about it, I thought. I shook my head in the dark. Sheesh, I wasn't even sure if I believed in God anymore. I certainly no longer believed in Mormon teachings about prayer. The doctrine went that a person was supposed to study the problem out in their mind, make a decision, and then ask God if their decision was right. If it was in fact right, they'd feel a burning in their bosom. If the decision was wrong, they'd experience a stupor of thought instead.

In all my years praying as a Mormon, I'd never once felt either a burning or a stupor. I was always left simply not knowing the answer. Did that count as a stupor? Perhaps that meant every single decision I'd ever prayed about was wrong. But the odds seemed against it.

I heard Mickey cough in the bedroom. I hoped he wouldn't get up yet. For some reason, I knew then that I'd have to go to work. There was no further sound and I relaxed.

Okay, so I'd better pray, I decided. First, the study part. I already knew about the penalty for skipping work on a Monday.

Plus there would be Mickey's disapproval to live with. And Mondays downtown were always bad anyway because so much work had piled up over the weekend. If I waited until Tuesday to go back, the workload would be even worse. All good reasons to go in today.

And the reasons for playing hooky?

I wanted to.

Besides, in the big scheme of things, what difference did it really make? Even if this were a sin, it was certainly a minor one, and everyone was entitled to sin a little bit once in a while.

No. I was supposed to become perfect.

Good grief, Tim, I told myself, stop being so Mormon. It had been over twenty-five years since Mickey and I had moved in together and been excommunicated. Was I ever going to get over it?

"Heavenly Father," I prayed in the darkened living room, snuggling under my blanket, "I've decided to skip work today. Is that the right decision?" Please, I thought, enlighten me.

I waited, but of course I felt nothing.

Not like the other day. I'd definitely felt something when my co-worker Fred talked to me Friday at the printer. "I was reading slave narratives the other day," he said. I thought it odd that a young white man from Idaho would be reading this kind of material, but I was also grateful he was stepping outside his comfort zone. Was he doing it because he knew I was married to a Black man? Being out at work really did make a difference. "You know," he went on, "back in the 1930's when so many writers were out of work like everyone else, the government paid some of those writers to interview old Black people and record their stories of slavery." I nodded. "What really surprised me was how many of them missed it. Missed it! Makes you wonder, doesn't it?"

I hadn't known what to say. I was shocked he would say such a thing with a Black co-worker just one desk over, someone who clearly overheard every word we said at the printer. I'd spluttered, "Well, even some gays are homophobic. Even some women believe they deserve less than men."

Fred had gone back to his desk, and I'd been upset all weekend about what he'd said. I wanted to be a Monday morning quarterback. I wanted to say that living in the midst of a Depression, after decades of Jim Crow, and forced to take menial, backbreaking sharecropping jobs that paid pennies, it was natural that Blacks hadn't found life after slavery the paradise it was supposed to be. The fact that some oppressed people weren't jumping for joy about their freedom said a lot more about the limits to that freedom than it did about their superior life as slaves.

I needed to tell Fred that today. Only I didn't want to go downtown at all, for that reason or any other.

After a few minutes, I prayed again, "Heavenly Father, should I go in to work today?"

I waited again but still felt nothing. Well, it wasn't a fair attempt, I thought. You couldn't vote both ways and expect one side to win the election. I looked at my watch in the thin beam of light filtering in from my office. It was 5:40. Time for my banana, but I didn't even want to get up for my banana. Let me rest my eyes just a few more minutes. If I missed the bus, I reminded myself, I could always catch the next one.

When I awoke later, it was 6:10. The sky outside was still dark. I felt a little better and thought that with just one more short little nap, I could get up and finish getting ready. But skipping work sounded so wonderful. Did I really have light and darkness battling for my soul? What would I even do if I did stay home? I had no desire to do any household chores. Mickey would be busy in his workshop and have no time to do anything with me. I'd end up bored and watching reruns of *The Golden Girls* on Logo. It would be better to go to work.

I closed my eyes. I was so comfortable here on the sofa.

At 6:35, I looked at my watch again. Normally, I'd be at work in just fifteen more minutes. I had to make up my mind. We had a rule that we couldn't simply email that we were going to be out. We had to call and talk to the manager in person. She usually arrived by 7:00. If I called, I wanted to do so before she arrived, so I could technically obey the rule but not have to talk to her directly.

Subterfuge had to be a sin. It was wrong to skip work today. Anyone could see that. Who needed God to tell me?

I should go. I should go. I should go.

But I wanted to stay home. For no real reason. I wasn't even sleepy anymore. I had just gotten the idea in my head and I couldn't get it out. I wanted to stay home.

I heard Mickey cough in the bedroom again and stiffened. I had to make a final decision now. Heavenly Father, I want to do the right thing. I always want to do the right thing. But I just want an extra day off. Can I please have an extra day off? Please?

Nothing.

Why did I even still believe in God at all when there was so much evidence he didn't exist? Or if he did exist, that he just didn't give a damn? Why couldn't this just be my decision and my decision alone?

Guilt was a horrible thing. It was a manmade scourge on humanity. I hated the Church for that. I hated all religions for the crap they taught.

But I wanted to go to the Celestial Kingdom, not some lower degree of heaven, when I died. I had to be *good*.

I shook my head.

The whole problem was that I hated work so much, even on a good day. It was just sucking my life away. I did it because I had to, despising every minute of it. My job was...it was downright slavery. I bit my lip for using the word even only in my mind. I had no right to use that word. I had no right to expect Mickey to work harder.

I wondered if his expecting me to always pay the bills by myself was his subconscious attempt at getting reparations. Or even if the attempt was actually subconscious.

I wondered, after all these years, if every time Mickey was fucking me, if he was really *fucking* me.

I went back in my office and started an email to my manager. "I'm going to be out today, I'm afraid," I began. "I'm not sick, but my husband is, and he needs me to do some things for him today." That sounded more believable than saying I was sick myself. I thought about saying I had to go to the bank for him, to the drugstore, and to drop off a bid at a client's house, but I'd read somewhere that if you were too specific in your lies, it was more evident you were in fact lying. I'd leave it at that. I added, "I'll call you shortly since I know you prefer phone calls when we have to miss."

I picked up the phone, dialed, and cupped my hand to shield some of the sound, hoping not to disturb Mickey through the wall, and left a message for my manager. I hung up and listened for sounds of stirring from the bedroom. Nothing. I breathed a sigh of relief.

I went back to the sofa and snuggled under my blanket again. It was done. No need to worry and debate and fret. It was done. It was done. I was free for the day.

Liars went to the Telestial Kingdom, I remembered.

Stop it!

I tried to rest on the sofa, but I was now completely awake. What was I going to do? Listen to Pandora all day? Maybe I should clean the bathroom. Dust. Weed the garden. I should at least be productive.

Goddammit, I was going to loaf today and that was all there was to it!

Back in the Church, I always believed that it was a weakness to doubt. But perhaps that wasn't where the problem lay. Maybe it was a weakness *not* to doubt.

It was all about doubting the right things.

I closed my eyes but then heard the sound of Mickey's fingers rummaging about in his Altoids bin. I realized I hadn't turned on his coffee yet and went to the kitchen. I pulled some frozen sausages out of the freezer and started heating them on the stove. Mickey always liked sausages for breakfast. They were almost ready when I heard the bedroom door open.

"Good morning, sweetie," I said as he walked into the kitchen.

"Are you sick?" he asked.

"Nope. Just going in late. Thought I'd fix you a treat this morning."

"Thank you." We kissed and then he poured himself a cup of coffee. I sure wished he didn't drink coffee.

As Mickey started to eat, I went back to my office and put on my work clothes. I returned to the kitchen, grabbed a banana, and then, after kissing Mickey goodbye, headed out the door.

Reverse Engineering

"Dear Rhonda," I emailed, "I have something very important to tell you. I have to ask your forgiveness for a terrible crime that I've committed against you."

It was my job in reverse engineering that first gave me the idea. I was spending the bulk of my waking hours taking products developed by other companies, mostly overseas, and breaking them down to find out how their designs were superior to ours, and then handing the information over to our own engineers. It had felt like discovery at first, a grand adventure, but by my third year at the company, it had begun to feel like stealing. Deceit. Sin. Lies.

It made me break down my own belief system to find out how it was made, and when I saw all the parts laid bare, it no longer seemed like a product worth inventing. That's when my quest began.

Born and raised in Spanish Fork, I'd served my obligatory mission in Minnesota, where I'd baptized three people. That was ten years ago. I'd felt like a failure at the time but was now grateful for the meager head count. I felt it my duty after my epiphany to tell them I'd lied to them, and then apologize for bringing them to Mormonism. One of my coworkers was in AA, and he'd explained the premise of making amends to all I had offended, and first on my list were the three converts I'd unwittingly deceived.

The first convert was easy enough to find. Rhonda and I had kept in touch these past ten years, through email and Facebook and Christmas cards. We'd flirted a little while I was a missionary, and even though she had since married and had two kids, we still flirted a little in our correspondence. She'd confided some doubts to me over the years, and then I'd confided a few of mine, so I was sure this would be the easiest convert to address and therefore chose her first.

"I am now completely aware that the Mormon Church is a fraud," I continued my email. "I was an adult when I met you, even if a very young one, and have to take responsibility for my actions. I deceived you. There is no other way to say it. Others were involved and are responsible for their parts, but I am accountable for mine. I can't tell you how sorry I am for how this has impacted your life. I do apologize and hope that someday you can find it in your heart to forgive me."

Her response arrived in my inbox less than two hours later. "Ray," Rhonda wrote back, "I am deleting your name from my email address book. I am unfriending you on Facebook. Please do not try to contact me again."

I understood her hurt at having been deceived. She had every right to be angry. Then I continued reading. "I pray that one day you repent before you die and are thrust into Outer Darkness for all eternity because of your arrogance."

Wait a minute. Was it pompous to apologize? She wasn't mad because I lied to her. She was mad because she still believed the lies. But she had told me so many times about her doubts. What was going on?

I frowned at the computer and then shrugged. Her reaction was certainly disappointing, something I would only have expected from a true believer, which she had led me to understand she wasn't. But I'd done my part. I'd tried to make amends.

Still, if I'd gotten someone fired from a job, then they'd become homeless, and I merely apologized, that would hardly be making amends. That would only be trying to assuage my own guilt. But what could I do to actually make Rhonda's life better? Any further contact on my part would basically be stalking, another crime for which I'd have to make amends. Her response wasn't much of a resolution for either of us, but there was really not much else I could do about it.

I had been responsible for driving competitors out of business with my reverse engineering. There was no real way to atone for that, either. In the past few weeks, I had submitted resumés to various other companies for a new job that wouldn't require me to cause so much damage, but I was still going in to work every day while I waited for an interview. Could you really commit sins knowingly and then repent later? Was repentance even an option under those conditions?

The second convert I wanted to contact was Mort. He'd been about twenty-two back during my mission days, just finishing college, and he'd moved shortly after his baptism. I put his name in WhitePages for every significant city in the entire state of Minnesota but nothing came up. I vaguely remembered hearing Mort talk about wanting to live in Canada someday, and just on a whim I checked out Calgary and found his name.

Maybe I was being guided by the Spirit.

Just because the Mormon Church wasn't true didn't mean there was no God.

I called Mort one evening around 7:00. "Mort," I began, "my name is Roy Hughes. I was the Mormon missionary who baptized you ten years ago in Minneapolis. Do you remember?"

There was a chuckle on the other end of the line. "You guys don't give up, do you?" he said, laughing. "I had my name removed from the records years ago, and you all keep trying to pull me back in."

"You're not a Mormon anymore?" I asked, dumbfounded.

"I was just trying something new at the time. You know how kids are."

"When did you resign?"

"About a year after I left Minneapolis."

"So you're not mad that I baptized you?"

Mort laughed again. "I didn't say that," he replied. "If I'd had any idea how tenacious you guys were, I'd have never invited you into my apartment in the first place."

"Well, I *am* sorry," I said. "That's why I'm calling. I'm contacting all the people I baptized to apologize."

"Are you going to contact every kid you ever taught in Sunday School, or all the adults you taught in Sacrament meeting?"

I hadn't thought about that. I suppose he was right, though. My talks and lessons to hundreds of people over the years had led to their further indoctrination. Did it really matter if I apologized to a mere three out of all the people I'd influenced?

"I suppose I could stand up in Fast and Testimony meeting one last time before I'm excommunicated," I said, "but one two-minute talk before I'm yanked off the stage would hardly counteract the hours and hours of talking I've done before."

"Well, I still appreciate your call," said Mort, "but Elder Hughes, *don't* call me again."

He hung up, and I was left trying to decide if that attempt to make amends had actually worked or not.

Now I had one more convert to locate. His name was Case, unusual enough that I was surprised I couldn't find anything online. Even an obituary should have shown up, shouldn't it? After three nights of countless hours on the computer, I finally decided to hire a private investigator. Maybe I couldn't atone for every person's life I'd influenced, but I could do these basic three. That had to count for something in God's eyes. I was sure there was still a God.

It took Mr. McKay of the McKay Agency only two days to find Case. "I'm afraid I've got some bad news," he told me when I went to his office for the report.

"He's dead?" I asked. How horrible. He'd died a Mormon, still believing the deception. I was sure that whatever God was out there, though, was completely understanding. Any God worth worshipping loved everyone. It was just that dying under a delusion felt so…so unfulfilling.

"No," said the detective, "he's not dead, but he may as well be. Turns out he left Minneapolis to attend Brigham Young University, and while there, someone found out he was gay, and he ended up undergoing electroshock therapy."

"But BYU stopped that years ago," I said, not surprised to learn Case was gay. I'd suspected it even at the time. It was one of the reasons I was so happy to bring him into the Church, where I knew his soul would be saved.

I could feel the bad taste in my mouth.

"In any event, the subject fell into a deep depression and tried to kill himself." Mr. McKay paused. "But he didn't succeed. He's been in a coma for the past eight years. Some occasional movement, but it doesn't look good. I can give you the name of the nursing home."

My mouth fell open and I stared at the detective. My actions had completely and horribly ruined a man's life. Permanently. Forever.

I'd been so proud of myself as a missionary, sure I was doing the Lord's will, but what I'd done was destroy another human being. Was it pompous to feel responsible? Or was it the least I could do?

While I still believed in God, I wasn't so sure about Jesus. It wasn't clear there was any way I could ever be forgiven for such an atrocity.

"Thank you," I said. "Yes, please write down the name of the nursing home for me. And could you find out if his parents are still alive?" I wasn't sure apologizing to his parents would help or not, but it was obvious that had to be done as well.

It was the following day when I received a call from my mother. "Ray," she said, sniffling into the phone, "you keep telling everyone these past few weeks that the Church isn't true. Haven't you heard the story about the person who cut open a feather pillow and let the wind carry off all the feathers, and then had to try to gather up all the feathers again? You're like that man. Every time you lie about the Church, you have a feather you'll never be able to collect again."

For a brief second, I felt guilty, and it was that second of self-doubt that made me angry. "It's all the self-loathing and guilt and fear of life I've spread that I'll never be able to gather back up again," I said.

"Ray, we've put your name on the temple prayer roll. And your Dad and I are fasting for you every week. Your brother and his wife, too. Even Gram and Gramps, at their age. We all love you."

"I'm leaving my job in Belmont and moving to Provo," I said. I was done with Silicon Valley.

"You—you are!" Mom gushed happily, sputtering in surprise. "Oh, our prayers are answered! And we only just started fasting!"

"I'm going to get a job as a nursing home attendant," I said. "I can do that for a few years before my savings run out."

"And maybe you'll find a nice Mormon girl there."

I liked girls enough, but I'd decided a long time ago I was never going to marry. "I'll be reading gay novels to a man in a coma," I said.

Mom had no words to reply.

"Maybe I'll even read him some porn."

Mom started crying, and I realized I'd have to make amends for this too one day. Was there no way not to hurt others as one made one's way through life? How was a person supposed to live with that heavy burden every day of their existence?

"Oh, Ray," Mom was crying.

I supposed I could lie and tell her everything she wanted to hear. But that felt too much like reverse engineering a relationship. Sometimes, you just had to make your own product, regardless of what your boss or your competitors thought. Even if that made you unemployable.

"I love you, Mom," I said, "but I've got to go." I hung up and Googled the nursing home in Provo where Case was living. I gathered all my relevant information and filled out their online application. The man I converted could eventually be assigned to me, and I could visit him for a bit every day after work. I thought about how unpleasant the coming years were going to be as an ex-Mormon in Utah County, and I had a sudden thought. My Mom had always acted out of the sincerity of her heart, and I was fully aware of that. If I didn't blame her for all the grief Mormonism had caused me, why should other people blame me?

I wasn't sure, but what I did know was that there was a difference. Mom didn't realize, even now, the magnitude of her complicity. But I was fully cognizant of mine.

There was a difference.

Was I being pompous?

I went on Amazon and started browsing through gay novels, spending the next hour picking out four I thought Case would like, one that promised explicit scenes of anal sex. Maybe I could excite Case back to life. If there was a God.

I put all the books in my cart, selected Free Shipping, and then hit Submit.

Sweating Bullets

"So, Xander," said my companion, Elder Brediger, to our investigator, "do you think you could come to church this Sunday?"

Please say no, I willed him. Please say no.

"Sure, Elder," replied Xander. "It's time I finally see if the marketing matches the reality." He chuckled.

My heart sank. This Sunday was Fast and Testimony meeting. Most missionaries loved getting investigators out for this particular meeting, but I tried to avoid it if at all possible. I didn't find the Spirit especially strong when the members were left to bear their testimonies in an unstructured environment. And the ward where I was presently serving seemed unnaturally populated with odd members. Elder Brediger and I had worked so hard teaching Xander, and now we were likely to lose him.

"Why did you invite him for *this* Sunday?" I asked my companion after we left Xander's apartment.

"Transfers are coming up in just over two weeks," he replied. "Either you'll be transferred, Elder Osborn, or I will. We've been together three months already. And I want this baptism to go on *my* record. We don't have any time to waste."

"You'd have had a better chance of getting Xander baptized by waiting another week," I returned. "Now he probably won't be baptized at all."

"Why not?"

"Haven't you been paying attention to Fast and Testimony meetings the past few months?"

"Yes?"

"You don't think our members are…a little weird?"

"Elder Osborn, they're all children of our Heavenly Father. Stop being so judgmental."

I let the subject drop, mostly because Elder Brediger was right. But I was still right, too. Was it possible for two different ideas both to be right at the same time? I shrugged as we climbed into our car. We'd find out in just two more days.

Missionaries were not allowed to fast more than the first Sunday of each month, but I began my fast a little early on Saturday, begging Heavenly Father to let the following day proceed without embarrassment. Xander was a good guy, thirty years old, with a good job, a good mind, and a good personality. The Church could really use someone like him. Like Elder Brediger, I wanted him to be baptized, too, and if my companion was right in pushing him this quickly, after only four lessons, then the world would be a better place. I'd been out here in Indianapolis nine months and had only baptized four people, all back in my last area. If we baptized Xander, it would boost my spirits, boost the spirits of the ward members, help the mission stats, and finally get me promoted to senior companion.

Plus, Xander would be on his way to exaltation.

But Fast and Testimony meeting in *this* ward? I just wasn't sure. The members talked about their vacations, bore their testimony of the beauty of a flower, talked about their generosity in giving seventy-five cents to beggars at intersections, gave reviews of the latest Deseret romance they'd read, and talked of the lessons they'd learned from embroidery. One man had gone on at length about the blessing of having toenail fungus.

Maybe other people felt the Holy Ghost during these meetings. What I felt was uncomfortable.

Sunday morning came soon enough, and Elder Brediger and I waited in the lobby until just before 9:00. Maybe he wouldn't come, I hoped. Maybe the Spirit told him to wait a week.

But at 8:55, Xander came strolling into the building. "Good morning, Elders," he said cheerfully, shaking our hands. We introduced him to a few people and then hurried into the chapel before the doors were closed. Elder Brediger led us to a pew about midway toward the front. We scooted in beside a family with four young children, each with their own bag of Cheerios, and I watched the mother sneak a Cheerio herself, hoping no one would see her transgression.

We had some announcements, an opening song, a prayer, and the sacrament, and then the moment of truth began. Please, Heavenly Father. Please.

Sister Walker was the first to speak, as usual. She was an elderly woman with bleach white hair who seemed to feel that she was due to keel over dead at any moment and wanted the bearing of her testimony to be one of her last acts. "I look forward to the day I can see my beloved Stanley again," she concluded, "and I say this in the name of Jesus Christ. Amen."

Whew, I thought. Dodged a bullet. Maybe today wouldn't be so bad. I looked over at Xander, who was observing the meeting with a slight detachment. Detachment was better than horror, though. I'd take it.

Next, Brother Diggs from the High Priests group went to the microphone. He was about fifty, with graying hair and a slight paunch. "Brothers and Sisters, I'm very grateful for all the blessings Heavenly Father has given me." He paused. "In fact,

I've written a song about how I feel, and now I'd like to sing it to you."

My heart stopped beating.

Then Brother Diggs began. And it was awful. The song had six verses, and Brother Diggs had the voice of a pygmy piglet. I loosened my collar. I wished I weren't wearing this suit jacket. My underarms were so damp. I looked over at Xander. He was covering a smile with his hand. At least he was amused, I thought, thanking Heavenly Father for the assistance. Most of the people in the chapel kept looking at their watches.

Finally, though, Brother Diggs finished his song. I thought that would be the end of the ordeal, but he then continued bearing his testimony another three minutes.

I hated Fast and Testimony meeting.

Brother Hoover stood up next, from the Elders Quorum. He couldn't have been more than thirty but was already mostly bald, not an attractive look on him, especially since his torso was so long that his shirt kept coming untucked from his pants. "I want to tell you all about the way Heavenly Father interceded in my life this week," he said. "Yesterday, I had to fix some plumbing in my kitchen, and I just didn't know what to do." All I could think of was his plumber's crack. It was not a pleasant image. "I was afraid I'd have to tear up the entire kitchen, and Samantha was just beside herself. So I prayed. And do you know what?" He paused to let everyone guess in what miraculous way God had intervened. "Heavenly Father helped me remember where the pipe I needed was behind the drywall, so I only had to cut open a small hole. Right behind the sink." He shook his head in wonder. "It was a miracle." He nodded now. "Miracles *do* happen today."

Oh, my heck, I thought. Please sit down. You're embarrassing yourself. Brother Hoover actually began crying then but after only one more painful moment, he returned to his seat. I wiped my brow.

I couldn't bear to look at Xander to see his reaction. I kept looking straight ahead. Please, Heavenly Father, don't let anyone crazy get up there. Please.

Ann strode quickly to the podium next. She was in her late teens, graduated from high school but still living at home, with no job. The bishop was trying to encourage her to go on a mission. She had terrible acne and what people generally called "an attitude problem," but the sister missionaries visited her regularly, trying to inspire her.

"So most of you know I have a problem with drugs," she began, and I wanted to crawl underneath my pew. "The court ordered me to go to this rehab program, and I want to tell you, it really strengthened my faith in the Church."

Maybe this wouldn't be so bad, after all, I thought, straightening up in my pew.

"The first day, the leader came into the group, drinking *coffee*." She let the disdain drip from her lips. "*He's* supposed to help and show me the right way?" She laughed, a bitter sound. "*My* addiction isn't nearly as bad as his. The Word of Wisdom doesn't say anything about crack, you know."

This was the end of the world, I thought, as Ann continued. Xander could never feel the Spirit after a testimony like that. I could feel the sweat rolling down the sides of my chest. But I had to know. I stole a glance at Xander and saw him staring at Ann with his mouth open.

She returned to her seat, and I saw everyone looking at their watches again. The mother sitting near us sneaked another Cheerio. Then Harold walked to the front of the chapel. Heavenly Father, I prayed, aren't *you* supposed to be in charge? How can you let Satan ruin this meeting? Harold was a nightmare even on a good day. He was tall, overweight, unattractive, gangling, and had no social skills. Why he even wanted to get in front of an audience, I didn't know.

"I want to say that I know the Church is true," he began. "Heavenly Father answered my prayers and gave me a girlfriend this week. She's not a member yet, but she's really awesome." Harold continued for the next few minutes, describing the girl in question. I felt torn between being happy for him and wishing he would hurry up and finish. Then something unbelievable happened. His cell phone rang. And he answered it.

"Hi, Tina," he said, still standing in front of the microphone. "No, I'm still at church. I told you. No, not till 1:00. I said not till 1:00. I'll meet you at Cindy's at 1:00." He put his phone back in his pocket and continued talking to the congregation.

Oh, my heck. Oh, my heck. Oh, my heck. Would this meeting never end?

Harold continued talking, now about how Heavenly Father had helped him find a rare comic book he'd been seeking for years. I was going to have to take my suit jacket to be dry cleaned. The young man seemed just about to wind up when something horrific happened. His cell phone rang again. And he answered it another time.

"Hi, Mom. I'm busy right now. No, I told you I was going to see Tina today. No, I won't be home for lunch. Yes, I know it's Fast Sunday, but I'm having lunch with Tina. Mom, I've got to go." He hung up, said some words about Joseph Smith, and finally, finally, walked away.

Heavenly Father must not want Xander to be baptized, I realized with a certain degree of sadness. I had really hoped he might become a member. I felt such a wave of sadness at the realization, but then a fighting spirit sprung up from deep within. Heavenly Father, I prayed, we're almost finished. Please, please, *please* let the last speaker bring down the Holy Ghost upon us all. You can do this, I prayed, realizing I was being a cheerleader. You can do this.

I breathed a sigh of relief as I saw Brother Simmons walking slowly to the front. He was the former bishop, and most of the congregation wished he were still in office. He did try to correct the current bishop in public sometimes, to show that he knew more than the new guy, but overall, he was a decent man. Finally, I thought, finally.

Brother Simmons talked about his recent trip to the hospital for a kidney stone, and how the peace of the gospel helped him through a very difficult time. He calmly and rationally bore his testimony of Jesus Christ, of Joseph Smith, of the Book of Mormon, and of the Church. Then he concluded, "And while I suffered nigh unto death with my kidney stone, I know my suffering was probably only half of what Jesus Christ suffered in the Garden of Gethsemane. Jesus sweat blood, but I sweat stones."

I gasped, and I heard the same sound come from several others in the congregation. Had this righteous man just said what I thought he said? I looked about, and several others near me were looking about in shock and confusion as well. Xander actually turned to me and stared at me with furrowed eyebrows. We'd lost him.

I'd told Elder Brediger, hadn't I? Now we'd have to start all over with someone else from scratch. And poor Xander would never see a baptismal font. He'd never marry in the temple. He'd never make it to the Celestial Kingdom.

Finally, gratefully, mercifully, the closing hymn and closing prayer were done, and we all stood up. The mother near us sneaked one last Cheerio before heading to her next class.

"So, what did you think?" asked Elder Brediger, slapping Xander on the shoulder with a big grin.

Had he not been in the same room as the rest of us?

Xander shook his head, and I braced myself. He wouldn't even want to stay for the rest of the meetings now. I forced a smile, too, and waited for his response.

"I just don't know what to say," he began. "I was expecting something completely different." He shook his head again. "These are real people here, not fake like in most churches. These are people who really need what you have to offer, really need each other. It's quite refreshing."

Elder Brediger looked at me and smiled. I'm sure my smile had been replaced with an open mouth.

"Where do we go next?" asked Xander.

"The investigator's class," my companion replied, leading the way down the pew toward the aisle. "We still have a lot more we'd like to teach you."

Xander nodded and followed Elder Brediger, and I followed in stunned silence behind them both. Maybe the Church really *was* true, I thought, mingling with the other members as we slowly trudged back toward the foyer. I looked about me and shook my head, holding onto my scriptures tightly. There was a lone pink jelly bean on a pew beside me. I snatched it up and slipped it into my mouth, asking Heavenly Father to continue his mercies and send his spirit down to the investigator class as well.

The Contract

"Bishop," I said, trying to keep my voice even, "I need help understanding why Heavenly Father allowed Carter to die." My only son had been murdered a month ago in the basement of our home where we'd set him up in his own apartment. On Mother's Day. Jim, my husband, wouldn't discuss what had taken place. The neighbors looked at us in fear and avoided us. People at church whispered and put on sad faces, but no one would talk to me. "My Patriarchal Blessing promises that I would have grandchildren, that my son would take care of me in my old age. I have a contract with God. I want to know how such a thing could happen."

"Heavenly Father can't stop evil men from being evil," he said in a smooth, comforting voice. It wasn't comforting. "Perhaps you should have had more than one child."

I stared at him.

"What I mean to say," the bishop continued, "is that perhaps you were too close to your son, babied him too much."

"What in the world does that have to do with him being murdered?" I asked in confusion. Priesthood leaders were supposed to be inspired. This man in front of me spent his days as a bank manager. Even the apostles were mostly attorneys and businessmen. Mormon Church leaders could do with a little training. More than just a religion course or two at Brigham Young. "Are you saying if we'd charged him more rent, he'd still be alive?" Sometimes, I thought my bishop might have Asperger Syndrome, but he seemed to catch my sarcasm. I didn't want to be difficult, but I was under a lot of stress, and he was spewing nonsense.

The bishop closed his eyes and swallowed, looking as if he'd just eaten a raw snake egg. A rotten one at that. "Sister Gibson," he said, "I don't want to make the situation any more difficult for you than it already is, but you must know that your son associated with...unpleasant people."

"My son was a junior at the University of Utah," I replied. "He was an English major."

"So you understand what I'm saying." The bishop looked relieved.

"What in the world are you talking about?" I demanded. Maybe I should speak with the stake president instead. Of course, he was really just the owner of a small chain of restaurants here in Salt Lake.

The bishop sighed, looking as if he now realized he was talking to someone mentally deficient. It was the look he often had when he spoke to me. In the past, I'd just accepted it, but today I wanted to scratch his eyes out. My son had been murdered, and this man was patronizing me.

"Do you know what Carter told me in one of our interviews?" the bishop asked.

"I have no idea," I replied, "since you haven't said anything specific yet."

"He told me he learned that Shakespeare wrote love sonnets to another man." He shook his head. "He told me he *liked* those sonnets."

"Everyone likes Shakespeare's sonnets," I replied. "What's your point?"

"Carter told me that he read a play by Oscar Wilde. *The Importance of Being Earnest.*"

"I don't understand what you're talking about. Carter read dozens of plays and poems and novels. He was an English major. We already established that."

"Carter told me he liked that play. He told me...he told me it was good and funny. He told me being gay couldn't be a sin because a sinful person couldn't have written something so wonderful." The bishop paused, looking at me as if he'd just added two plus two and was hoping I could make the intellectual leap to come up with the answer all on my own. "Sister Gibson, your son was becoming corrupt. He started accepting gays. He started thinking like an *intellectual*." He sighed. "He started going down a path that could only lead to destruction."

I smoothed the skirt over my knees. "Bishop," I said carefully, "I came to you for help. My son has been murdered. In his own home. In *my* own home. And you tell me he brought it on himself because he read books?" Now I was beginning to wonder about the bishop's intellect.

"Sister Gibson," the bishop replied, "you're aware, of course, of the covenants we make in the temple?"

"Are you kidding me? I go once a month."

He nodded. "We are making a contract with God. We promise to obey him. We promise..." he said, "we promise to live chaste lives."

My brows furrowed. "Are you telling me my son wasn't chaste?" Now I was confused again. "Carter told me just a week before he died that he was still a virgin." I stopped and took a breath. "He told me he was afraid he'd die a virgin. And he did." The thought made me sad, but I'd promised myself I wouldn't cry in front of the bishop.

"Sister Gibson, you're making this very difficult. I want to honor your son's confidences, but I feel you're pushing me to reveal the true nature of some of our talks."

My son had been a good man. An Eagle scout, a returned missionary who'd been a zone leader in his mission to Maine, Gospel Doctrine teacher in his Singles ward. He went grocery shopping with me every week and helped me understand which products were the best buy, either for price or for quality. He read me poetry during Family Home Evening while Jim was watching Monday Night Football. He still had Family Evening with me, not with the Singles in his ward. He was a good boy.

"Sister Gibson, your son was gay." The bishop breathed a sigh of relief, as if he'd just said something important.

"Well, of course he was," I replied. "I've known that since he was six years old." Was the bishop telling me Heavenly Father had allowed him to be murdered because of *that*? "He was also committed to living the gospel. He was a virgin," I repeated. A mother made a contract with her children, one literally signed in blood, to watch over them. I'd made sure Carter was a good man, whatever burdens the Lord had placed on his shoulders. "It's not a sin to *be* gay. The Church has said so. It's just a condition, like having epilepsy or being sterile." I bit my lip, remembering how I'd never been able to become pregnant a second time. "A burden the Lord gives to test us."

The bishop shook his head. "Your son came to me many times," he returned, "agonizing over his situation. He said the temptation to sin was too great, that celibacy wasn't an option, that he wasn't strong enough to live an entire life without falling, that he knew he was damned."

I didn't know what to say about this revelation. It seemed unlikely, but surely the bishop wouldn't lie at a time like this. Yet it still didn't explain anything.

"I told him to watch a lot of LDS movies," said the bishop. "I told him to read LDS books." He looked very sad. "And do you know what he told me?" He paused, and I wasn't sure if he was expecting an answer. "He told me they weren't very good. Can you imagine?" He looked as if he were about to try to reach over his huge desk and touch my hand, but then the moment passed. "Your son was corrupt," he repeated.

"Bishop," I said slowly, "I hear words coming out of your mouth, but I don't understand what you're saying. Are you telling me my son was murdered because he didn't like Deseret Book?" I thought back to one of the last activities Carter and I had shared together. We'd watched a DVD of *Sister Act* one evening. I remembered him telling me that since it was about nuns, it couldn't be a sin to watch. I'd thought it an odd remark at the time, but he must have been feeling guilty for watching any regular movies at all. I wanted to slap the bishop for making him feel that way. The bishop was supposed to be giving him strength, not making him feel like a failure for watching a simple comedy about a church choir. Even if they were Catholics.

"I made your son sign a contract," the bishop continued. "To remain celibate for six months. I was afraid to make the contract for any longer than that. I thought we'd take it a day at a time. But Carter came to me not a month after he'd signed it and told me he'd been to a gay bar."

I took in a deep breath.

"He said he didn't go home with anyone," the bishop assured me. "He said he only drank a Coke, but he said he saw a cute guy..." The Bishop swallowed. "And he went home and masturbated." He closed his eyes. "Your son was in serious trouble, Sister Gibson."

I nodded, finally starting to understand the gravity of the situation.

"Your son masturbated all the time. At least twice a week. I hate to have to tell you all this. I don't want to mar the memories you have. But as bishop I have the power of discernment, and I sense you need to know the truth."

I looked down in my lap for a long moment before turning back to the bishop. I picked at a piece of lint on my skirt. "I...I still don't understand," I said. "Are you saying that Heavenly Father let him be struck down because he was evil? You keep telling me he wasn't the good man I thought he was, but I still don't understand how this has anything to do with his being murdered."

The bishop clasped his hands together and blew out a heavy breath. "I don't think you appreciate the severity of your son's depravity. You know he was a stake missionary."

"Yes?"

"He came in to tell me that one night when he was going on splits with one of the elders, the missionary told him he was homesick and cried." The bishop looked very uncomfortable. "The missionary put his head on Carter's shoulder, and Carter hugged him."

I felt uncomfortable, too, but I also felt proud of my son for being decent. It wasn't a sin to be decent.

"Carter came into my office, and *he* cried. He said it was the first time he realized that it was intimacy with another man that he really craved, not just sex. He was heartbroken because the missionary wouldn't talk to him again after that, because he was too embarrassed. Carter was very hurt."

I looked at my lap again. I'd come to the bishop for understanding, and I was finally starting to get the bigger picture about my son's life. Maybe the man *was* inspired. Now I felt sad and hurt and happy and confused. Carter had been a good person. Even all these "revelations" did nothing but prove that. I was sorry for his pain but grateful he had remained true to the end. Perhaps Heavenly Father hadn't punished him by allowing him to be murdered but had actually done him a favor, kept him a virgin until the day he died.

"Do you know what your son told me during our last interview?" asked the bishop.

It couldn't be bad, I told myself. It couldn't.

"He told me he wanted to kill himself, but he was too chicken. He said he was a failure even at this, and it upset him greatly."

I thanked God that my son had been murdered and hadn't committed suicide, an unpardonable sin. I was glad I'd come to see the bishop. He was making me come to terms with the murder. I saw now that it was God's doing. I breathed a sigh of relief. The bishop was a good Latter-day Saint. The Church was a great institution, even with untrained lay leadership. I'd wondered sometimes, but now I knew. The Church was true.

I wished Carter had come to me about all this. I would have read poetry back to him. I could have helped him through it all. That's what mothers were for. I could have been more emotionally intimate with my son, given him what he needed. He would have been okay.

"Carter told me he tried to tell your husband he was afflicted with same-sex feelings," the bishop went on. Now he looked uncomfortable again. "He told me Jim cut him off when he sensed the direction the talk was going, that he said he'd rather hear that his son was dead than that he was gay."

My mouth hung open. The words stung, but I knew the bishop was telling me the truth. That sounded like exactly the kind of thing Jim would say. In fact, now that I thought about it, I remembered that Jim had been especially tense and moody that last week before Carter was murdered. He'd slammed doors, broken a plate, been very rough during sex.

Oh, my Lord. "*Jim* didn't kill our son, did he?" I put my hand to my mouth.

"No, no, no, no, no," said the bishop, horrified. He looked up at the photograph of the First Presidency on his wall as if asking for guidance. He seemed to want to crawl underneath his desk rather than go on. But what could there be left to tell? "Carter," he said slowly, as if every syllable pained him, "Carter said that he was a failure even as a gay person because he didn't know any bad people. He told me...he told me..."

"Yes?"

"He told me he was going to go to the sleaziest bar he could find and..."

Oh, my Lord, I prayed, don't let him tell me Carter had sex before he died. Not when he only had a few days left to live. Heavenly Father, please don't let him tell me that.

"Carter said he only had $250 to his name."

"He didn't hire a prostitute, did he?" I asked in horror. Oh, why had I come in to talk to the bishop? Why hadn't I left well enough alone?

"He told me he was going to hire a hit man. Take a contract out on his own life." He shook his head. "Of course, I thought he was joking."

I remembered now what the police had said. Carter had opened his door and been shot immediately in the head. There had been no robbery, no apparent motive of any kind. They'd asked if Carter had been into drugs but gave up when they found nothing incriminating in his apartment. Nothing except an unsigned love letter. I'd thought it might be from a girl. Finally. But now I suspected the young missionary. Some of the previously vague references now made sense.

"Sister Gibson, your son committed suicide."

I looked the bishop in the face for a long moment, and he looked back. He seemed about to try to reach for my hand again. I looked up at the photo of the First Presidency as he had done. Then I stood up.

"I appreciate you taking the time to talk to me," I said. "I understand everything perfectly now." Carter had given me the best Mother's Day present a child could give his mother. The gift of dying before he was hopelessly lost to the Adversary. The suicide we could work around, since he hadn't pulled the trigger himself. It wasn't a sin to make the ultimate sacrifice to protect one's virtue. Girls were told that all the time. It had to be true for gay men, too. They were almost like girls, weren't they? "You haven't told the police, have you?"

"I thought it best not to, under the circumstances." He turned his palms upward in supplication. "No sense besmirching your name. Or the Church's."

I nodded. "Thank you, Bishop."

He stood and offered his hand. "Please come talk to me any time you need to," he said.

I shook his hand and started for the door but turned back. "Well, I have been having some difficulty with one of my teachers in Young Women," I said. "I'd like to talk to you about Sister Bingham sometime."

"Does next Sunday at 1:00 work for you?"

"That'll be fine." I smiled, a weak smile, but my first real one in several weeks. "See you then." I walked out the door, down the hall, and out through the lobby entrance. I climbed into my car and turned on the ignition.

Tonight I wouldn't complain if Jim was rough. I'd made a commitment to him in the temple. I was lucky he was a real man. One always had to defer to the priesthood. I was lucky to have so many good priesthood holders in my life.

Even Carter. Maybe what he did *had* made him a real man in the end.

I thanked Heavenly Father for all my blessings and headed home.

Third Time's the Charm

"Betsy, you're seventeen, and it's high time you got your Patriarchal Blessing." My mother wagged her finger at me. I was lying on my bed trying to concentrate on my chemistry homework. I glanced at the poster of Rosalind Franklin on my wall.

"All right, Mom. I'll talk to the bishop this Sunday." I'd been thinking about it anyway, but I'd let Mom believe she'd convinced me. She liked feeling she was saving me. My soul was good enough, I supposed, though I preferred science books to General Conference, and French lessons to Seminary class. I never missed church, though. Janet, another one of the Laurels, was getting a blessing soon. And I'd heard that Rachel over in the next stake had gotten one a few months ago. I needed to call her one of these days and catch up.

"I just wish we had two patriarchs in this stake. Some stakes have two, you know."

"I'm sure one man can be as inspired as two."

"Three would be even better," she continued.

"Well, there are three people in the bishopric," I agreed, "and three people in the stake presidency. And three people in the First Presidency."

She nodded worriedly. "I just wish we could choose our leaders sometimes," she said. "We have no choice in what ward we go to. Or what bishop we have. Or what stake president we have. It would be nice for such an important event as getting a Patriarchal Blessing to allow *some* choice. It's the blueprint for the rest of your life."

"Heavenly Father chooses for us," I said. "Doesn't he, Mom?"

She looked at me and frowned.

I talked to Bishop Jackson after services on Sunday, and he gave me Brother Curtis's phone number and told me to have my parents make an appointment. Two nights later, Mom drove me over to the Curtis's house. They were an older couple, and Sister Curtis stayed with Mom in the living room while I went in the back den with Brother Curtis for a talk, to allow him a chance to get a feel for my "spirit."

I got a feel for him, too. He asked me lots of questions, personal ones, and seemed genuinely interested in my answers. I wish my parents acted like that. Maybe this wasn't going to be so bad, after all. I did wish he didn't call me Janet twice, though. But he seemed like a nice enough guy.

Still, I had a flashback of a scene from the movie *Ghost*, with Whoopi Goldberg scamming her clients. "Black suit?" "Could be blue."

I clearly needed the guidance this man could give me. Before my teenage cynicism became adult apostasy.

I was grateful that my mother wasn't allowed in the room. My blessing was going to be personal, between me and Heavenly Father. I could share it with others if I chose, or I could keep it to myself and just ponder it alone in my room. After we talked for a good twenty minutes, Brother Curtis turned on the recorder, smiled, and then stood behind me. When I felt his hands resting on my head, I closed my eyes and waited.

Would I hear I'd win the Nobel Prize one day? Would I be told I'd hold the priesthood? What wonders in my future was Heavenly Father going to prepare me for today?

It started out safely enough. I was declared to be of the lineage of Ephraim, as was almost everyone else who received a Patriarchal Blessing. I had kind of hoped to be from one of the Lost Ten Tribes. Then a few other generalities began. "You will be a faithful daughter of Zion. Because you were valiant in the first estate, you've been blessed with a fine mind and an excellent physical bearing."

I wasn't quite sure what he meant by that. I was certainly an A student, except in P.E., because I was a muffin top and preferred to read over playing sports. But maybe it meant I would blossom later. The possibility of being beautiful one day made me smile. I hoped that comment wasn't a generality. I couldn't wait to read the printed version later.

"You will hold many important callings in the Church, but your most important calling will be that of a wife and mother in Zion. You will have sons and daughters who will praise your name."

Plural. Both words. That meant at least four kids. Damn.

"You will first be called to serve as a full-time missionary, a calling that will help you prepare for your eternal marriage to another Latter-day Saint who will also have served a mission. You will face many hardships and trials, but you will grow in righteousness and spiritual strength."

Brother Curtis continued slowly in a monotone voice, the words just dragging out of him, and the warmth in the room and the comfort of his hands, plus my closed eyes, made me start to doze after only a few minutes, despite knowing I was hearing a prophecy regarding my own life. I needed to stay alert. Even if I was going to be given a printed transcription in a few days, I wanted to hear the patriarch's tone of voice as he pronounced future events. That tone might give me additional clues. Only the tone continued in that horribly monotonous manner. Why had I eaten such a big dinner before coming over? I just couldn't stay awake.

Several minutes later, I opened my eyes and realized I'd missed something. But the patriarch was still speaking. "You will have great success in your career. You will be a mentor and be highly recognized in your field."

The sleep evaporated instantly. A Church leader was telling me it was okay for a woman to have a career, and that I'd be good at it! This was news. Maybe now my parents would help support me in college. As I continued listening, I searched for actual details, but so much of what Brother Curtis was saying *almost* sounded specific but never quite was. And even though I was desperate to hear more about my work, I soon found myself dozing again.

When I awoke later, Brother Curtis was talking about my children. "Your oldest son will have the personality and bearing to achieve great things in the world of politics. Your oldest daughter will be a great help to you with the younger children." He went on to describe the personalities and contributions of all the children, listing six in all. Here he was at his most specific. My youngest son, for instance, was going to become a great leader in the Church. Of course, I didn't know if that meant bishop, stake president, or actually one of the General Authorities. It was still a little vague, even while trying to be specific.

I stole a glance at my watch. The patriarch had been speaking for almost forty minutes! The few blessings I'd read from friends had been only two to three pages long. Mine must be twenty pages by now. I must be an incredibly special spirit, I thought. Perhaps I should pay more attention at church. I certainly needed to pay more attention now.

Brother Curtis spoke for another five minutes, saying more things which were even less clear than earlier. There was something about my "staying abreast of world events" and "seeing the signs of the Last Days." Did that simply mean I'd subscribe to a cable news channel?

"You will counsel others in difficult times." So should I interpret that to mean I was going to hang out a shingle during Armageddon, or merely that I would give advice to a friend who'd argued with her husband over which color to paint the bedroom? It was all tantalizingly vague, but I enjoyed thinking of the possibilities. It was kind of like Nostradamus, whom we'd studied briefly at school. His prophecies were always crystal clear...*after* they'd come to pass.

Finally, though, the patriarch concluded with the words, "I promise these blessings upon your head in accordance with your faith and diligence in keeping the commandments. You will have a good and full life as you base your decisions upon gospel principles. And I say this in the name of Jesus Christ. Amen."

He lifted his hands off my head and took a step back. I stood and thanked him, shaking his hand, and then I went out to meet my mother. "Good grief," she said on the way to the car. "I thought you had died in there. What took so long?"

"Apparently, I'm special."

She looked at me and frowned. I'd heard stories that perhaps Brother Curtis acted too familiar with some of the teenage girls, yet he'd been nothing but professional with me. Of course, I was in the middle of a break-out right now, and my puffy flab was more obvious than ever in the outfit I wore tonight. But

Church leaders would never be inspired to put a lech in a position where he would be alone with young women anyway.

The patriarch had spent so much time with me because I was extraordinary. Maybe I should try harder to be Valedictorian. Perhaps I should join the Math Club.

Maybe I should finally start fasting on Fast Sunday.

I couldn't wait to read the transcription. Sister Curtis would type it all up. Then I'd get a copy while another copy would be stored somewhere in the Church archives. I could spend hours reading and reflecting and praying about it, preparing for my future. I'd wondered about serving a mission, to learn a language if for nothing else, but now that decision was made for me. I had to go. It was prophesied. And I knew my husband had to be an RM. And I knew I couldn't start using birth control until after I'd had six children. I was surprised to realize how comforting it was to have so many of the difficult questions decided for me. The blessing really was a blessing.

But Bishop Jackson called me the next evening. "Betsy, I'm afraid there was a problem with your Patriarchal Blessing."

"What?" I asked. Had the patriarch been talking about someone else and given me the wrong blessing? He'd seemed awfully focused on Janet in our get-to-know-you talk. She was certainly more vivacious than I was, and scheduled to come in the following evening, tonight. Perhaps he'd been tuning in to her future and not mine.

"It turns out the recorder was broken and didn't record the blessing. Brother Curtis will have to give you another one."

My mouth fell open. All those wonderful things he'd said. Were they lost forever? Surely not. If he was inspired the first time, he'd be inspired again.

The only reason Joseph Smith didn't retranslate the lost pages of the Book of Mormon was so that no one could alter the stolen portion and claim he wasn't translating them again the same way the second time. But there was no one to cause trouble here. My blessing would remain the same.

Only it didn't. When I met with Brother Curtis the following Tuesday night, we repeated our get-to-know-you talk to refresh his memory, and then he put his hands on my head a second time. I'd drunk some caffeinated Coke before leaving home so I'd be sure to stay awake this evening, and things started off well enough. I was still of the lineage of Ephraim. That was good. But this time there was no talk of my serving a mission, no talk of my career. I was still going to have six children, but there was nothing specific about any of them. When the patriarch concluded, I looked at my watch.

Ten minutes!

Where had the rest of my blessing gone?

I marched out angrily and met my mother in the other room, and we walked back out to the car. "What happened?" she asked. "Did he do something?"

"Let's just go home, Mother."

I slept fitfully that night and awoke exhausted, but I had a chemistry test at school that day and forced myself to study one last hour before the exam. I was sure I'd aced it. That helped my mood a little, but the following evening, I received another call from Bishop Jackson. "Betsy?" he said. "I've got some more bad news."

"For the love of Pete," I said. "What happened this time?" I stomped my foot. I needed to exercise Christ-like patience. Perhaps this was all a test.

"Someone broke into Brother Curtis's home and stole the recorder, among other things. You'll need to make another appointment."

In the midst of my irritation, I realized this might actually be a sign of Heavenly Father's intervention. Maybe this was God's way of getting Brother Curtis to redo it right on the next go around. Heavenly Father wanted me to have the full forty-five minute blessing again. The burglary was probably a punishment because the patriarch had been shirking his duty with me last time.

So on the following Tuesday, I was back at Brother Curtis's house. My mother stayed to talk with Sister Curtis in the living room while I went back with Brother Curtis in the den. We had yet another get-to-know-you talk, and I specifically mentioned my plans to go on a mission and to do well in my career, to refresh his inspirational memory. And then he lay his hands on my head again. I had a surreal feeling I was practicing the Scientific Method, repeating an experiment to test the results.

I was still a descendant of Ephraim, I was still a choice daughter of Zion, I was still going to marry in the temple, I was still going to have "good children," but that was about it. The entire thing was over with in just five minutes. Five minutes!

As Brother Curtis smiled and shook my hand, I began to wonder if any of this really meant anything in the first place. Maybe it was all smoke and mirrors.

Though even Oda Mae Brown turned out to be real in the end.

Maybe something would happen to this recording as well. And next time, I'd insist on seeing another patriarch. Surely I could receive permission to talk with the patriarch in the adjoining stake. Perhaps that's what Heavenly Father had in mind the whole time.

I called Rachel when I got home to get the scoop on her patriarch. She and I only saw each other at regional events, but I did have her phone number. "Hi, Rachel, this is Betsy. From Springfield Ward."

"Hey! What's up?"

"Are you happy with your Patriarchal Blessing? I know you got one a while back, but we never talked about it." There was silence on the other end of the phone. "You still there?" I asked.

"My blessing says I'll have sons and daughters," Rachel replied.

"Yes?"

"I already found out a year before I met with the patriarch that I'll never be able to have kids."

"Well, maybe there will be some medical breakthrough," I said.

"I don't have a uterus anymore," Rachel replied.

"Oh." I thought for a moment. "Maybe it means during the Millennium. Or after the Resurrection."

"I suppose," Rachel conceded, "but the Patriarchal Blessing is supposed to tell us about our actual life, not about our afterlife. It doesn't tell us what kingdom we'll go to, does it? Or tell us how many sister wives we'll have in the Celestial Kingdom. Or tell us about the planets we'll create."

"In Seminary, someone told us about his cousin whose Patriarchal Blessing said he'd go on a mission to a 'strange land,' but he died before he turned eighteen. His parents then realized there aren't actually any strange lands on the Earth. We know them all. So his blessing was saying he'd go on a mission somewhere else. Your blessing might be the same thing."

"Well, it's not very useful to hear about something that won't happen until after I die. A Patriarchal Blessing is supposed to help us get through *this* life."

"Maybe...maybe your stake patriarch just isn't inspired. Doesn't mean they're *all* bad. You can get another blessing from someone else. That's what I intend to do."

Rachel laughed. "You can't shop around," she said. "You get what you get. I haven't been to church in two months."

"Oh, Rachel."

"The patriarch didn't see *that* coming."

We talked a few more minutes, and then I hung up. It wasn't right to let my faith falter just because Brother Curtis wasn't a great man. There were lots of Mormons who weren't the best people. Like Rachel. That didn't mean *I* had to fall away. I could only achieve greatness in my career if I had Heavenly Father on my side. I wanted his help and so I was going to be good. But I needed his blueprint in order to do that.

I'd heard that people could recall memories through hypnosis. Perhaps I'd find a therapist who could help me remember that first session. At least the parts for which I was awake. That would be something.

There was no call from Bishop Jackson the next day, and I wasn't sure if I was grateful for that or not. I started reading more of the Book of Mormon at night after I finished studying for school, and I waited anxiously for the authorized copy of my blessing to arrive in the mail. When it did, I ran up to my room and knelt beside my bed to pray. "Please, Heavenly Father, help me to see your hand in this."

I opened the envelope and began reading. Two lines in, I saw, "You are of the blessed tribe of Manasseh." I stopped for a second and reread the line. Then I hurried through the rest of the two pages.

This wasn't even my blessing. It was even more generic than what I recalled from our last meeting.

My Patriarchal Blessing was a form letter.

Brother Curtis had given up after three attempts and just pulled out something from his files. I sat on my bed staring at the paper in my hands. I wanted a recount. I wanted to see another patriarch and bring my own recorder. I wanted to see the Prophet. I deserved some respect.

"Betsy, dinner's ready." I heard my Mom calling from downstairs.

"Be right there."

I sat looking at my blessing for a long moment, reading the empty lines. Glancing up, I saw Rosalind Franklin intent in her lab. Setting my lips, I slowly crumpled the letter and chucked it forcefully into my Big Bang Theory trash can. At the door, I turned back and went to my desk, picking up my Book of Mormon, and dropping it in the trash as well. Then I went down to join my family for dinner.

Your Mission, If You Choose To Accept It

"Uh, I don't feel so good," said my companion, Elder Marks, putting his hand on his stomach. "Do you mind if I use your bathroom?"

Antonio motioned toward the hallway leading deeper into the apartment. There was a large crack in the wall from the earthquake in November of last year. 1980 had been the death date for over three thousand people in the Napoli area, but in some ways it was the year of my birth. I felt so much more alive out here in Italy than I had back in Scottsdale. Every day was an adventure, stopping people on the streets, knocking on the doors of strangers, eating dinner with new contacts. We were eating spaghetti alle vongole tonight, something I'd never had before. Elder Marks stood up from the table with his hand still on his stomach and hurried down the hall. Antonio looked at me and grinned. How embarrassing for Elder Marks.

"Anziano," Antonio began. "No—Giuseppe—we have to talk quickly."

My name was Joseph Lucas, but as a Mormon missionary, I was simply called Elder Lucas for the two years I was on my mission. Yet it thrilled me to hear Antonio use the Italian version of my first name, like a code name. I felt so sophisticated speaking a second language. In some ways, I felt like a spy, living outwardly as a dedicated Latter-day Saint while having a secret life underneath that I hid from everyone, from my companions, the mission leaders, and especially the investigators I was trying to inspire. I fantasized about meeting someone who knew my secret, someone who could then call me on another, better assignment. But of course I would never really leave my mission. Or the Church, for that matter. It was just a fantasy I let myself dream, to add another layer of sophistication to my life. A shy reader addicted to Ian Fleming led a pretty pathetic existence, especially now that Ian Fleming was forbidden reading material. No movies allowed, either. When Antonio called me Giuseppe, it felt like we were sharing a secret. "Sí," I replied, "che c'é?" We were of course speaking Italian throughout the entire meal. I'd been out fourteen months, the last four here in Naples, and Elder Marks had been out five since leaving the Missionary Training Center. Even he could muddle through a conversation.

"Giuseppe, I put something in your companion's food to make him sick."

"What?"

"There was no other way to speak to you alone. You guys are always together."

"It's the mission rule. So we don't stray."

Antonio closed his eyes. "That's exactly what I want to talk to you about." He paused and I nodded for him to continue. Sometimes, there was a look about him that made me wonder if he led a double life, too. Elder Marks and I had tracted him out almost five weeks earlier. He was twenty-two and worked as a shoe salesman. At least, that was his cover, I allowed. We'd taught him all of our lessons, plus several invented ones to justify our visits. He'd only come out to church once and wouldn't commit to baptism, so this was going to be our last evening with him. Besides, when I'd called earlier to make an appointment to say goodbye, I'd told him I was being transferred tomorrow back up to Rome where I'd started.

"Giuseppe, I want you to move in with me."

I stared at Antonio in surprise. We'd always gotten along well. I really liked him and had told him so. Elder Marks and I had even invited him to go to the Capodimonte museum with us one P-day. And I'd also told him I had thought of studying Italian more thoroughly after I finished my mission, that I might even move here permanently, but I certainly couldn't get a roommate right now. I looked at him suspiciously. It seemed a strange invitation. Was he truly leading a secret life? Perhaps he was asking me to go undercover with him.

Undercover? I was such an idiot. I needed to focus a little more on reality.

Of course, Antonio *had* slipped something into the food. That was something Peter Graves on *Mission: Impossible* might have done.

"What are you talking about?" I said. "I still have ten months left." Still, to have the possibility of housing as soon as I was ready for civilian life again was intoxicating. I wanted to keep this feeling of sophistication. Having a secret life in Scottsdale felt so empty. If I had to have a secret life, I wanted to do it in this exotic country. And while Rome was cleaner than Naples, it was the people of Naples I really loved. They were so open and friendly, like Antonio. His olive skin promised...something.

Antonio reached over and put his hand on mine. That was another reason I loved Italy. Men could touch each other, show affection. I knew I could never really *be* with another man the way I wanted, but this was the next best thing. I'd insisted on continuing these meetings with Antonio for just that reason, even though Elder Marks had said three visits ago we should dump him.

"I want you to move in right now. I can't wait ten months."

"But you only have one bedroom," I replied. "Even if I did want to be roommates, we'd have to find another apartment."

"We only need one bed," said Antonio. I felt my hand trembling underneath his.

I stared at him, the way people looked at Barbara Bain taking off her latex mask and revealing her true face underneath. "Tu sei…" I faltered. "Tu sei…"

"Un finocchio. Sí."

"Flip," I said in English.

"What?"

I heard a loud groan come from the back of the apartment. "Is he going to be okay?" I asked.

"Probably."

"Antonio, do you know what you're asking me?"

He nodded. "I've been meaning to tell you for a while now, but I was afraid you'd stop coming over. But since you're leaving anyway, I figured I didn't have anything to lose."

"But I hardly know you," I protested. I didn't even ask how he could tell I was gay, too. I was always amazed no one had suspected yet, constantly afraid of being found out. I felt like I was meeting up with an ally in enemy territory.

"How long does it take to know you're in love?" Antonio took my hand and led me from the small kitchen table over to the sofa. It was covered in tan fabric that was fraying at the edges. He sat down and pulled me onto the cushion beside him. Now he held both of my hands in his lap. "You're handsome, you speak Italian better than I do, and I've seen the way you look at me. You want me, too. Don't deny it."

I shook my head. While all this was thrilling to hear, the truth was we *weren't* spies. We were ordinary people. And I was Mormon. What he was asking was impossible. "But we don't have anything in common," I said. "All I know is that you like calcio and I don't. Look at those posters on your wall." I nodded toward the two huge photographs of prominent Italian soccer stars tacked to his living room wall. One of them halfway covered another crack.

"I don't give a damn about soccer," he returned. "Those guys are up there because they're hot. But I'll take them down for you."

The world was reeling. I felt so dizzy. Was it another earthquake? I wondered if Antonio had slipped something into my food as well. Maybe he wasn't a spy for any Earthly country, but he must certainly be an agent of the Adversary. I heard an agonized grunt from down the hall. Were we both about to be murdered? Degenerates could do anything.

I looked at Antonio, who was staring at me intently. Then I looked at my hands in his lap. Where they shouldn't be. He saw my glance and pressed down on my hands. I felt…

Oh, my heck.

"Giuseppe, I know what I'm asking. It's hard for me, too. My family doesn't know, but they will if you move in. I'm willing to risk people finding out my secret. For true love. Aren't you willing to risk anything?"

"But I have the true church," I said. "You're not risking the same thing. I'm risking *everything*." Even I could tell I sounded like an ass. Why would this guy even want me in the first place? I was no Sean Connery. Or George Lazenby, for that matter.

Antonio leaned over, his face coming nearer and nearer. I knew what he was about to do. I should get up, I thought. I should run outside, even if it meant leaving my companion to fend for himself. I should...

He kissed me. I had never even kissed a girl before and didn't know what to expect. After only a few seconds, the first thought that popped into my head was, "So *this* is what everyone is always talking about." It was wonderful.

This was the kind of thing James Bond did.

The kiss lasted a long time. Or at least it felt like it did. But all too soon, Antonio was pulling his head back. "I know you know," was all he said.

I pulled my hands out of his lap and turned to face a soccer player with firm, hairy legs. "This is essentially the first date I've ever had in my life," I said. The two girls I'd dated a handful of times each certainly didn't count. "You can't expect me to marry someone after only one date." This wasn't a game, even if I did feel like I was playing chess with Kronsteen.

"That's pretty much what Elder Marks intends to do after he goes home, isn't it?" asked Antonio with a grin.

"It's...it's not the same."

Antonio sighed. "Giuseppe, we don't have much time." He looked down the hallway, which was silent now. "Please, when you leave your apartment tomorrow, don't go to the train station. Come here instead."

"Non posso," I said, hardly able to form the words. "I can't." I had always known I'd have to forego love in order to stay a good Mormon and reach the Celestial Kingdom. But now I knew it in a way I never had before. It was like the difference in *saying* you knew the Church was true, and actually *knowing* it.

Testimonies sucked.

I looked down at Antonio's crotch.

I wanted to be James Bond.

"You can teach English to make a few dollars until you find a regular job. I know it's hard to get work in Naples. And it'll be worse since you're American. We'll be poor. But it'll work out. You'll see. Have faith. You can have faith, can't you?"

"Antonio…" How could I have faith in sin? This wasn't some childish game, I told myself again.

Antonio grabbed my face with his hands. "Answer me this—do you love me?"

I looked at him and hesitated.

"Yes or no?"

"Yes," I said. "Yes." He smiled, and my heart melted. I would give away nuclear secrets for that smile.

But I wouldn't give up the Celestial Kingdom for it.

We heard the door to the bathroom opening. Antonio dug into his pants quickly. "Here's a key. I have to work tomorrow, but I want to see you here when I come home." He slipped the key into my hand, and I put it in my pocket.

"Elder Marks, are you feeling better?" asked Antonio, sounding sincere. Who could believe anything a guy like that said? He was an agent of Kaos. But a serious one. He wanted to destroy me, and then he'd kick me out on the street and laugh. The war between heaven and hell was a Cold War, and I didn't want to end up a prisoner in some god-forsaken cell.

"Anziano," Elder Marks panted, "we've got to go home." We picked up our scriptures and headed for the door.

"No prayer?" asked Antonio, a little sardonically.

Elder Marks flung open the door and hurried out. We would have a fifteen minute wait for the bus, and then another fifteen minute trip back to our neighborhood. I hoped we'd make it. We stood underneath the street lamp, Elder Marks with one hand on his stomach. Would Antonio do something like that to me one day? What if we had an argument about something? What if he wanted to break up? He was a classic villain. Worse than Blofeld. Even if he weren't asking the most outrageous sacrifice from me to begin with, he was in no way the kind of guy I could ever trust enough to live with.

And I didn't want to live with *any* guy. I wanted to marry a pure woman in the temple and have lots of happy children. Why was I entertaining his suggestion even for the merest tiny second? It was preposterous. I was a good boy. And I was going to stay a good boy forever. I wasn't going to lead a secret life. I was a Mormon, and I was going to live openly and honestly.

"I don't feel so good."

"Hang in there, Elder. We'll be home soon."

Thankfully, the bus came only a moment later, and traffic was lighter than usual, so we were home within a few minutes. Heavenly Father looked out for his own. And punished traitors. There would probably be another earthquake in Naples if I tried to see Antonio again. In fact, I should have dusted my shoes off when we left his apartment this evening. That kind of curse was not to be cast lightly, but if anything warranted it, this did. That wasn't a missile from a car, or a knife from a shoe sole. It was a real weapon, a weapon of the Spirit. I had to focus on reality before my delusions destroyed me.

We were back in our apartment by 8:15, way too early. If we didn't get caught by the district leader, though, we could say we got in an hour later. Elder Marks headed straight for the bathroom, and I went to our room. I had packed my extra suit, my shirts and garments, my second pair of shoes, my ties, and my journal and tape recorder already. I packed my color-coded colloqui and my copies of *La grande apostasia* and *Il miracolo del perdono* now. I would wear the same shirt tomorrow morning, as there was no need to be 100% fresh when I would spend the day transferring. Missionaries traveled light. Like spies.

I bit my lip for continuing the fantasy, even when I knew it was long past time to stop.

Everything I owned was in these two suitcases. Everything I owned except my soul. And I did still own that. But I would lose it forever tomorrow if I did what Antonio asked.

And yet...and yet...I'd been praying for this exact opportunity ever since I could remember. I loved Italy. I loved Italian men. I loved the language, the food, the music. The words to a Claudio Baglioni song kept repeating in my mind. And I wanted that secret life. But I loved my mission, too. I was one of the few missionaries who didn't bellyache every night. I *enjoyed* spreading the gospel.

Still, the whole point of having the gospel was to create great families. Here I had the chance to create the only family that would ever make me happy, and I was throwing it away.

But wickedness never was happiness.

"You okay?" asked Elder Marks, coming into the bedroom. "You don't look so good, either."

"Maybe we ought to get to bed before the others come home."

"I'm sorry I made you leave early. I know you liked Antonio."

"It's okay."

"Well, you have to get moving as soon as you wake up tomorrow, anyway, so maybe we had better hit the sack."

"Shall I offer the companion prayer?" I asked.

"Thanks." We knelt together in the middle of the room while I prayed, and then I turned off the light and we both climbed into our cots wearing just our garments. I'd never be able to wear garments again if I went to see Antonio. I *liked* my garments. It was a blessing when even your underwear reminded you to think of God.

It was like having a secret chip implanted in your arm.

Stop it, Joseph, I told myself. Just stop it.

Giuseppe sounded so much nicer than Joseph.

If I went to Antonio's tomorrow, 1981 would be my death date. I was only twenty. That was too young. I didn't want to die a spiritual death. I didn't want to end up in Outer Darkness with Satan. Even Antonio admitted he'd never lived with another guy before. We'd be sure to blow it even if we tried to make it work. I'd lose out on eternal life and still end up with nothing here on Earth, either.

No fool would make such a decision.

I needed to be an adult. I was no longer a teenager watching action movies with other kids. Reading books that only fulfilled the writer's juvenile dreams.

I'd take the first bus that came by in the morning and head straight for the train station before I had a chance to sin. You had to know your own weaknesses and work around them. That's what a real person did. Not some stupid fantasy figure. Heavenly Father would note this tremendous sacrifice and bless me. I might even become a zone leader. My family would be proud of me, instead of wishing that I was dead. I closed my eyes and tried to clear the sin out of my brain. I slept fitfully, the single blanket somehow not enough, even though it was only early September.

I said goodbye to the other elders at 7:00 the next morning and carried my two heavy suitcases to the bus stop by myself. I thought about making a quick stop by Antonio's just to brush the dust from my shoes. Perhaps Heavenly Father would make Vesuvius blow this time.

Instead, I cleared out a couple of drawers and put away all my things, changing into the jeans I usually only wore on Preparation Day, taking off my garments and going without. I swept the floor and washed some dishes from last night that were still in the sink. The ordinary had never felt so exotic. I straightened some books on Antonio's scratched bookcase and dusted his worn dresser. And by late afternoon I had a fresh salad on the table, with sugo cooking on the stove, when not *The Spy Who Loved Me,* but the man I loved came home.

Books by Johnny Townsend

Mormon Underwear
God's Gargoyles
The Circumcision of God
Sex among the Saints
Zombies for Jesus
Mormon Fairy Tales
Flying over Babel
Dinosaur Perversions
The Gay Mormon Quilter's Club
The Abominable Gayman
Marginal Mormons
Mormon Bullies
The Golem of Rabbi Loew
The Mormon Victorian Society
Dragons of the Book of Mormon
Selling the City of Enoch
A Day at the Temple
Behind the Zion Curtain
Gayrabian Nights

Johnny Townsend

Lying for the Lord

Despots of Deseret

Let the Faggots Burn: The UpStairs Lounge Fire

Latter-Gay Saints: An Anthology of Gay Mormon Fiction (co-editor)

Available from BookLocker.com or from your favorite neighborhood or online bookstore.

Follow Johnny on his blog, QueerMormon.com, or on Twitter: @QueerMormon

CPSIA information can be obtained
at www.ICGtesting.com
Printed in the USA
FSOW01n0813160415
6418FS